CHIDIOGO LILIAN EZEJELUE

Harmony Publishing
Plot 1 Emmanuel Anabor Street, Off Mopo Road, United Estate, Sangotedo,
Lagos, Nigeria
Tel: +2347032212481
publish@harmonypublishing.com.ng

ISBN 978-978-974-422-0

Printed In Nigeria

Dedication

In memory of Chinazaekpele Francisca Ezejelue. Everything has changed but my love for you remains constant. Rest well, nwannem.

Acknowledgments

Odega Shawa, you pushed me to share this with the world, you helped me handle the hard stuff. I could never thank you enough.

Ucheoma Ezebuiro-Ossai, my Sisi, thanks for making me believe in my abilities.

Obi C. Fortunatus, thank you for the medical insight you so freely shared.

Victor Nwoko, I'm humbled by your faith in me and your desire to see me grow.

I am ever indebted to Immanuel James Ibe-Anyanwu. Words will not do.

Thank you Emmanuel Anyanwu for your words of encouragement and advice.

My parents, Mr Fred Nwoye Ezejelue and Mrs Chika Jacinta Ezejelue. I am who I am today because of the opportunities you two gave to me. Even when it was hard, you gave, and you continue to give.

Joshua Chukwudum Ezejelue, my brother - for reading over my shoulder while I wrote and making me feel like you were reading the best story of your life.

My siblings: Chioma Jacinta Ezejelue; Chiagoziem Ezejelue; Ebubechukwu Fred Ezejelue; Chidindu John Ezejelue, you were there from the beginning, you will be there till the end.

Prologue

efore I knew who I wanted to be, I already knew how my life was expected to pan out. It was supposed to go in this order: university education, National Youth Service Corps, and marriage during or after youth service. It was important that I be married at no later than twenty-three years old. It was also important that I marry a Catholic man from my home town and begin the vital task of procreation before my first wedding anniversary.

No one sat me down to read me this order or state it explicitly, but it was always hinted at from the moment I could communicate, such that it became part of my own expectations.

Another expectation that was made clear enough was that I could not date while in school. I also had to marry as a virgin.

We all knew this – my sisters and I – but as the Ada, the first daughter of the family, it was clear that I had to set the example.

For this reason, my parents cut me no slack when it came to discipline. My life was occupied with activities that prepared me for this life; one hour after-school lessons immediately I returned home from school, domestic chores, church activities consisting of choir practice and the compulsory daily evening Mass, all carried out under the watchful gaze of my mother. The aim, I suspected, was to keep me busy and focused.

There was also the yearly mmechi aho, held to celebrate the end of the year by my town folk living in Lagos. During this event, I had to make efforts to socialize, especially with the males, but in as subtle a manner as possible so as not to come across as loose and untrained.

I had a problem with attending this yearly event. Unfortunately, it was not an option as far as my parents were concerned. Prior to my teen years, I loved mmechi ahọ parties and began to anticipate one once we got into the 'ember' months. However, as I grew older, I began to feel like a product being inspected for purchase at this end of the year party where the youth were explicitly encouraged to mix and mingle.

Whoever was the Chairman at the time, during his speech, would say something along the lines of: "Look around you. We have beautiful, young women in our midst. What are you young men looking for in other towns that we don't have here?" And as advised, the assessment would begin.

Those who married ndi mba, someone from a different town, were made to look like sell-outs. Sell-outs were the products of parents who did not train their children well in the ways of our custom. It was up to me not to disgrace my parents in this way.

I was aware of these and had no intention of offsetting the balance which my parents and ancestors had maintained piously. I was a dutiful child, travelling in the straight path set before me, until the events of one rainy day caused my life to veer off course.

Chapter One

Every young girl around me looked forward to their sixteenth birthday. It was a big milestone, second only to one's eighteenth birthday. Sixteen was believed to be the age at which one had the best of both of life's stages; childhood and adulthood. At this age, one still has the radiance and vitality of children while also going through the physical development that bestows upon them the attractiveness of adults. There's also a bit of freedom too. People often refer to a beautiful woman as "sweet sixteen" and I believed it was because a woman is at her most beautiful at age sixteen.

At thirteen, I eagerly waited for the years to fly by so I could be sixteen. I expected a massive transformation to take place in my body as the years went by and that day neared. When passing a glass door or mirror, I would subtly assess my reflection, especially the curve of my backside and breasts. So far, there was little difference, but I expected all that to change as I neared my sixteenth year.

On the morning of my fifteenth birthday, the first thing I did was to look in the mirror, expecting some changes, no matter how small, an indication that in a year's time, at sixteen, I would be the curvy, beautiful woman I always envisioned, but to my disappointment, I looked and felt the same, the only curves on my body that grew bigger were the pimples on my cheeks. This bothered me to an extent as I went about my normal routine for that day. There was the hope that perhaps I could not notice the change in myself but others would and for most of that day I expected compliments, held my breath for them, but they were not forthcoming.

When school closed that day, I did not feel interested enough to partake in the compulsory rehearsal going on in preparation for the dignitaries visiting our school in a week. I asked for permission to leave immediately, claiming ill health. Not only was I exempted from the rehearsal, my class teacher also assigned a classmate and friend, who lived on the same street with me, to take me home.

Soon after we left the school compound, I regretted my decision as it began to rain heavily. I brought out the umbrella that was always in my school bag and handed it to Kehinde, who was slightly taller, to hold over our heads.

In my early years, I was afraid of the rain. Once the sky darkens and lightning streaks across the sky, I begin to imagine horrible occurrences; like the world ending in a gruesome manner, the ground opening and swallowing people, buildings collapsing, people being swept away by flood. I stayed away from the rain as much as possible. I did not mind looking through my window at the children playing in the rain and tilting their heads upwards with mouths open to catch raindrops, as long as I was within the safety of home. Not once did I join in their games and I was content with that.

I could not remember when that fear left me, but the thought that it was gone crossed my mind as I pushed my small hip against Kehinde's much larger one, and reached for the handle of the umbrella she was holding, pulling it close to my side. She dragged it back and we both jostled for the small umbrella which barely kept more than our hair dry. We laughed loudly and I wiped water off my face as we jumped the puddle at the entrance to Efutide Street where I lived for years. A heavy breeze blew then, howling like an animal in pain and nearly lifted the umbrella away. Reaching up with as much force as I could manage to counter the effort of nature, I struggled to hold the umbrella in place, but the wind was not giving up yet and curved the umbrella upwards, wetting our hair.

We squealed. Not our hair! It was just Monday and we had until Friday to wear the two-step hair style. A cat call followed our cry, drawing my attention to the wooden stall by the side of the street - and the men in it. Though most of their frames were hidden by the stack of biscuits displayed on the table before them, it was easy to see that they were both slightly built from the hollow in their cheeks. One was Ibrahim. I knew him well, but the other was a new face.

"Yarinya, I fit mend your ambrella," the new face said pointing at my now useless umbrella, then at some disused umbrella parts scattered on the floor outside the kiosk.

I ignored them but Kehinde tossed back. "Aboki, I am not your wife. Go and find another Yarinya."

Ibrahim and his friend seemed to find this funny. "No be you we dey talk to o. Na the other lepa one wey fine well well," the new face replied between bouts of laughter. I hissed at them and walked on but, within, my spirit soared because they thought me attractive.

Lightning flashed through the sky and, almost instantly, the sound of thunder had us covering our ears and running faster. As though the weather gained joy from our distress, the sky sent more rain and wind, taunting us.

Old No. 6. New No. 11.

We made a dash for the gate beside the rusted letterbox on which was written my house number and I gave the small gate a nudge. It opened immediately and, before I could catch it, swung all the way in and backwards, making a loud bang as it hit the other parts of the iron gate.

My head was bent all the while against the rain, so I could only see so far in front of me. I blew water from my lips, then gingerly jumped another puddle between me and the steps leading to the corridor of my home. As I started to climb the first step, I looked up to behold a pair of boots.

Kehinde's parting words went unanswered as I gazed into the beaming face of Obinna.

He was dry, untouched by the rain, and that squelched the instinct to run up and hug him. I remained standing at the foot of the step. His much larger hand enveloped my small one to pull me up the two steps to the corridor. They were warm and for the briefest moment, I wished they could cover every part of me and drive away the chill.

Suddenly feeling self-conscious, I squeezed water off the tip of my wet hair and adjusted my skirt at the waist before asking, "What are you doing here?"

"Won't you open the door and go inside? See how your teeth are shaking."

I reached for the key in my school bag. Every attempt made to get the key into its hole failed. The cold made me shiver uncontrollably. As I made to try again, he pried the key from my hand and let us in.

Once inside, I turned to him again. "I asked your mummy last week and she said you won't come back till Christmas. What are you doing at home?"

"You look like a wet rat. Go and change first, biko," he pushed me gently towards my room and, though stung by being likened to a rat, especially considering how unattractive I was already feeling, I went in obediently.

When I returned to the sitting room, he was sitting comfortably like he was a part of the house. To an extent, he was very much a part of our family - has been for as long as I can remember. My parents often regaled my twin sister and me with stories of how, apart from my parents and the hospital staff, his were one of the first eyes to behold us when we were born. I had heard the story over and over again, so many times that I could tell it the exact way my parents have told it over the years.

Obinna's parents left him with my parents to attend a function in a nearby state and it was at that time that my mother went into labour. With no one else to look after him, my parents took him with them to the hospital.

As we grew older, he spent as much time in my home as he did in his and I also could be found in his home whenever I was not in mine. He was the only visitor who could come into my house and put his feet on the centre table as he was doing at that moment.

My eyes left his feet to settle on a parcel wrapped in red and gold coloured paper. I reached for it, smiling as I picked it up from the table and began to tear it open.

"Who told you it's for you?" he asked from behind me.

"It's my birthday, of course," I eyed him over my shoulder and continued wreaking havoc to the wrapping paper.

"It could be for Ama."

Obinna and Ama were close but not as close as he and I were, so, since I could only see one package, I knew he got it with me in mind. In the previous years, he either got us separate gifts or got us one substantial gift and asked us to share.

"Well, she isn't here, besides…" The rest of my statement was cut off as I beheld what the package revealed. Quickly, I lifted the lid to be sure it was not a trick and, sure enough, there sat a navy blue Nokia 3310 mobile phone. I had wanted a mobile phone for quite a while, but my parents refused, insisting that I had to finish secondary school to be allowed to own one. I had begun counting the months until graduation and it seemed so long. All of a sudden, I was holding a phone, one that was all mine.

"Oh my God!" I managed and turned to find him standing behind me. Bereft of words, I flung my arms around him and squeezed tight. Outside thunder rumbled menacingly and the wind howled, but inside it was peaceful. The warmth of his body and the strong fragrance of the cologne he has worn since he was old enough to start wearing one wrapped me in an embrace that made me feel secure.

Despite how speechless I felt, I knew I had to show my gratitude, so I eased back a little to do just that and was forming the words when his lips closed over mine. I froze, only for a short while, then my reflex took over. I returned the kiss, tentatively at first, then he took it deeper and I followed readily, my hands moving up his neck to his head as his caressed my back.

The shiver that went through my body had nothing to do with the cold. Simultaneously, warmth spread through me gradually, steadily, like liquid fire, moving through every inch and pore, but rather than burn, it soothed. I sighed and let go of myself, leaning into him. He, in turn, inched back, taking me with him to lean against the wall.

As we lost consciousness of what was going on in our surroundings, we discovered each other, inch by slow inch. His mouth abandoned mine and moved to my chin, tracing the outline of my jaw with as much devotion. I let my head fall backward and he grabbed the tails of my cornrows pulling my head further back to expose my neck to his mouth.

My knees weakened and nearly gave way, but his arms held me up. I thought nothing, I heard nothing. I only felt. A feeling so overwhelming I never wanted it to end. Then it did.

Alarmed, my eye fluttered open. Had I done something wrong?

"Your sisters…" His breath was uneven, so that the words were almost incoherent. It gave me pleasure realizing that I had as much effect on him as he had on me. "They'll be back soon."

I shook my head pulling him back to me. "Rehearsal," was my laconic reply and he did not question further.

His face broke into a sensuous smile. Tilting his head, he looked at me like he never had: from my face, lingering on my lips, down to my neck and further down. When his eyes settled on my small bosom, which had caused me so much displeasure while comparing with my friends' and finding mine lacking, I self-consciously folded one arm over my chest. Reaching out a hand, he pulled the offending arm away and continued his intimate assessment of my body. After he had had his fill, his eyes returned to mine. It seemed as though he were looking into me, like he could see inside of me.

"You are extremely beautiful; every part of you," he said reverently, in a way that left no doubt that he meant what he was saying, and the insecurities that had plagued me all day disappeared immediately, replaced by a wanton confidence I had never felt. It felt empowering and rooted out every trace of shyness in me.

Soon he was nudging me onto the three-seater sofa and I did not resist, though I knew I should. Before the years of moral training I had received could kick in fully, he reached for his phone and switched it off, effectively shutting out the rest of the world and the voice of reason. There, held in his arms and sheltered from the heavy rain hammering against my window, I lost my innocence to him and he lost his to me.

We moved as one. It was like a dance, but nothing the world knew of. It was our dance, created by us and fitting for our bodies alone. I was not sure if the spark of light that flashed behind my closed lids was from the lightning or from within, but I was not scared. I felt secure while he held me like he would never let go.

As passion heightened, the world outside darkened until it appeared to be night rather than day. I had a vague feeling that it meant the forces of nature were protesting against our actions, but I was past caring. I was with the boy I loved and nothing could ever go wrong. So I thought.

Chapter Two

When I did not get my period the next month, I was excited to be free from the excruciating pain and discomfort and happily shared with Ama who was born seven minutes after me.

"You are always lucky. Your period is never regular. Mine will come next tomorrow and I'm dreading it already." She had her back to me, but I could see her face through the mirror in front of which she sat, unravelling her plaited hair. Combs and cutting combs of different sizes were scattered on the writing desk which doubled as our dressing table.

"Enjoy your womanhood and stop complaining jare. Did we not wish to get our periods when others started having theirs and we were still late?"

She threw a fistful of her hair which had come off at me and said: "I didn't know anything then. If I knew any better I wouldn't have prayed for this trouble." She hissed then turned away from the mirror to face me.

"Since you didn't see yours last month and this month why don't you give me your pad? My own will not be enough." She tilted her head to one side then gave me the look she used whenever she wanted to beg for anything.

"No!" I said hastily before I could get tempted to give in to her. "I'm not giving."

She threw her hair band at me. "What will you do with all of them?

Are you planning to start selling pads? Or you are saving them for your future children?"

Done with her hair, she turned back to the mirror, frowning at her reflection. Her face contorted in pain as she forced a comb through hair that needed retouching. "Who knows, maybe you are even pregnant with them already, this one that you've not seen your period for two months."

Seeing my reaction through the mirror, Ama's eyes doubled in size and she turned sharply to face me. "What?" She wore an expression of alarm most likely similar to the one I knew I must have on.

I continued staring, shocked, my brain calculating, considering possibilities and discarding them. I considered when last I had missed my period for two straight months and couldn't remember. One month maybe, but never two months straight.

"Oh no, Ada." Ama left her perch by the bureau and hurried to the bed to sit beside me. I shared everything with her, including the identical looks, and she knew me almost as much as she knew herself. "You are scaring me. I know you well and this is not a joke."

I thought it best to pretend I was not rattled, at least until I was sure, but I was too scared to worry about how my fear would affect Ama. She took me by the arm and shook me hard, her eyes growing bigger. "You are scaring me. Stop it joor!"

"Ama, what if I'm pregnant?" I wanted her to tell me I couldn't be, to mean it and also be right.

"You can't be," she refuted immediately, then frowned, searching my face. "Or can you be?"

The answer must have been clear because she was soon wiping tears off my cheeks, tears I didn't know were there and she started crying too.

Ama and I came out for dinner swollen eyed. My sisters, already seated round the dining table, looked at us quizzically, and so did my father.

"What is wrong with you?" father asked through a full mouth.

"Nothing," we both answered quickly.

"Nothing? You just felt like crying?"

Nnenna snickered. "Maybe they were watching something sad on TV." We were forbidden to watch television on a school night, except it was the network news, so this assumption earned her a stern look from Ama. Defiant, she returned the look but fell silent.

"What have you been doing inside your room since?" Father pointed his fork at us.

I stammered, not sure what to say, but Ama was quick. "We were filling our JAMB form."

"Fill it carefully and make sure there are no mistakes. Any one you don't understand, you show it to your mommy." He stopped talking to swallow his meal, then said, "Won't you sit and eat?"

One look at the large mound of yam porridge with smoked fish and my stomach roiled in revolt. Ama was already reaching for a chair.

"I'm not hungry," I said.

Ama's hand stopped midway to the chair and in solidarity she said, "Me too. I'm not hungry."

"Sit down there and finish every single thing on that plate." My mother's command was uncharacteristically harsh that it startled me. I looked at her and her eyes drilled into mine. She was in her usual seat, beside my father. While every other person's plate was nearly empty, her meal was barely touched. Ama and I exchanged looks then sat.

Father, an auto parts dealer, flipped through a spare parts brochure as he chewed his meal. He didn't act like he noticed mother's full plate or her mood.

Gradually, my younger sisters were done eating. Offering their thanks, they went into the kitchen with their plates and returned almost immediately to watch the news.

"To your room, all of you," my mother ordered in a voice unusually stern.

Simultaneously, their eyes went up to the clock. Nnenna, who was always outspoken, voiced the complaint they all obviously had. "Mommy, it's not even eight o'clock."

Upon noticing my mother's foul mood, they stood, all four of them, and shuffled out of the parlour, grudgingly.

Soon after they were gone, my mother turned to my father and dropped a bombshell. "Ada is pregnant."

I gasped loudly and looked at Ama, though I knew she could not have told my parents because she had not left my sight since we both discovered just hours ago. She shook her head and raised her hands, palms out in defence.

I could not meet my father's gaze, too terrified of what I'll find there, but I looked at my mother, wondering how she knew.

"Ada, is this true?" Father's voice was dangerously calm.

"I don't know yet."

As soon as the words were out, a blow hit my cheek, almost sending me out of my seat to the floor. There was a loud buzz in my ear. I felt my bladder give way and wetness soaked through my trousers to the chair I sat on. There was nothing for it but to look at the source of the blow. My father looked nothing like himself as he glowered.

"You don't know yet? Meaning you could be." He raised his hand to hit me again but Ama, who was sitting between us, blocked me and got hit instead. He turned to her.

"Are you pregnant too?" She shook her head, nursing her neck where the slap had landed.

"So this is what you two have been hiding?" Eyes blazing, he turned to my mother. "How long have you known?"

With her forehead supported by the palm of one hand and her eyes closed, she was a picture of dejection. Her elbow resting on the table shook slightly. "Just today. I was about to enter their room when I heard them talking about it."

She opened her eyes then and looked at me. They shone brightly with unshed tears. "Tell me, Ada, where did I go wrong? What did I do for you to choose to disgrace me this way, ehn?"

I couldn't talk through the tears and the weight lodged in my throat.

My father stood abruptly, placed his hands on his hips, and exclaimed loudly, his eyes darting around like a caged animal desperately looking for a way out. Ama reached for my hand under the table and squeezed, offering me strength, but for the first time, her presence was not reassuring.

Sitting back down, my father pinned me with his gaze. "Who is responsible?"

I was silent.

"Don't let me repeat myself." He raised his voice as he said that, causing Nnenna and the rest of my sisters to rush to the door.

"What is it?" As usual, Nnenna was the one to speak.

"Inside!" both my parents ordered and they scampered off. As soon as their bedroom door closed behind them, my parents' eyes settled on me again.

There was nothing to do but to tell the truth.

"Obinna."

"Obinna nwa Silas Onwuka?" Incredulity laced my father's question.

Father was protective of Silas Onwuka and his family, and I believe the feeling has always been mutual. From the moment my father, a young businessman new to Lagos, walked into First Bank in Marina to ask for financial advice and Silas attended to him, answering all his questions, they struck up an unlikely friendship. They were an unusual match; one a university graduate working as an account officer in a bank, the other a secondary school leaver running his spare parts business.

Their friendship continued even when they got married, extending to their wives and then to us the children. The bond between them became stronger as they grew in their careers and Mr Onwuka became a bank branch manager while father's business expanded to accommodate apprentices who came and went after they were done learning the ropes.

I could understand why my father found it hard to accept anything that'll cast the Onwukas in a negative light.

I nodded. "Yes, Uncle Silas' son."

"Don't you dare lie against that good boy," my mother warned.

"She is not lying." Ama came to my rescue again. "It happened the day he bought us that phone for our birthday."

"Hei!" My mother raised both hands to her head. "So phone is your problem, mgbo? Why didn't you tell me you needed a phone?"

I didn't bother reminding her I had asked for one on several occasions and was told I was not old enough to own one.

She stood immediately and stormed out of the parlour like one controlled by an unseen force. I heard the door to my room open then, seconds later, she returned with the phone.

"So for this you gave yourself away, nwa a?" She threw the phone hard against the wall and its parts scattered in different directions. "This is how little worth you placed on yourself? Hei! Chim o, what have I done wrong?"

My stomach rumbled and I ran for the toilet. My mother followed, running behind me. I thought she was coming after me to continue scolding, but as soon as I pushed open the door and bent over the toilet bowl, emptying my gut, she was beside me doing same. We both stayed that way, one giving way for the other to vomit. There was no strength left when I was done and I fell to the floor. Opening the tap, my mother rinsed her mouth in the bathroom sink, then, taking some water, she joined me on the floor and wiped my mouth. Once done, she guided my head to her shoulder and held me tight.

"I advice my students not to do this and then my daughter goes and does just that. What will people say when they find out that mother and daughter are pregnant at the same time?"

Shocked, I tried to raise my head to look at her, but her hand kept my head in place. Anguish washed over me and we both cried.

Stoic. That is the word that comes to mind whenever I think of Obinna's mother, Aunty Oyedinma Onwuka. She was always composed in every situation, no matter how daunting. Time spent in the courtroom over the years, representing clients, meant she had heard and seen more than most humans. Not much fazed her, so I was understandably concerned for myself and for Obinna when she began her call to her son without the usual pleasantries, proceeding instead to order him to return home.

"Obinna, you have to come home." The use of his real name, instead of 'Nna', her pet name for him, was another indication that she was deeply distressed by the bit of news my parents revealed. Her hand holding the phone shook visibly and her husband, Uncle Silas, patted her free hand resting on the sofa between them.

While she listened to her son, I watched her inhale and exhale deeply, several times, then she seemed calm once more and in control. When she spoke again, it was still with none of the endearments she usually interjected while talking to her son, but other than that, she was back to being the composed woman she was known to be.

"Your father is okay. You'll see everyone is fine when you return. It's just that something came up that I think you should be made aware of."

Obinna must have sensed something was amiss. From her reassuring words to him, I figured he had concluded that something was wrong with a member of his family, his father particularly, and my heart hurt for him. I wondered which could be considered a graver situation; a problem with a member of his family or being a father-in-waiting at only seventeen years.

"No, Obinna. You are coming home today. I want you here in the next two hours."

Her voice brooked no argument and I knew Obinna would be back in no more than two hours. No one disobeyed Obinna's mother.

The next two hours were the longest and most uncomfortable of my life. I spent it pinching the skin surrounding my fingers and welcomed the resultant pain, feeling like I deserved worse. My eyes kept going to the clock and, each time, it seemed the hand of the clock had barely moved from where it was the last time.

Almost two hours after the call, I heard Obinna's voice shouting excitedly from the front of the house.

"Uncle Sam, Aunty Chinyere, good afternoon."

He greeted my parents even before he got into the parlour to see them. Our Mercedes-Benz V-boot, parked within the compound, was obviously what informed him of their presence. Obinna would recognize my father's car wherever he saw it and even knew the car number plate by heart. It was the same with me. I knew all of Obinna's parents' cars and their number plates, all four of them.

As his footsteps got closer, I felt sorrow for him just thinking of what he was about to face and knowing that the delight that carried through in his words was about to vanish. Soon, the sorrow metamorphosed into trepidation. What if he denies my claim?

Whenever our families came together, one could hear their banter and laughter from a mile away. It wasn't so at that moment, so when Obinna parted the curtain to enter the parlour, he froze at the threshold and looked around, panic evident in his eyes. Our eyes met and I noticed that instant realization hit him. He bowed his head slowly.

"So it's true?" Obinna's mother, who knew her son's expression so well, sounded disappointed.

Uncle Silas lowered his head to his palms and said nothing.

"I trust you," was a statement Obinna's mother said often to us. Now, I could almost hear the unspoken *"you have broken my trust"* and that hurt me more than anything else. I saw that it hurt Obinna too.

Another thing that hurt me was the possibility that our indiscretion could sever a relationship between our families that was born long before either Obinna or I was brought into the world. The uncomfortable silence between our parents and the conscious effort made by all to avoid eye contact proved that animosity between both families was a possibility. My parents stood then and without a word they walked out with me in tow.

Chapter Three

"Your life, as you know it, is now over. Your dreams, your aspiration, all gone!"

I had always thought the principal's office too impersonal, with all the furniture in dull brown colour. Even the books on the shelf were mostly with covers in different shades of brown. The only vibrant colour in the room was the gold designs against the brown wooden award plaques and the gold cups our school had won. Everything else was depressing and each time I found myself in her office, I longed to get out.

When the result of a pregnancy test confirmed what we already knew and a meeting with the principal became inevitable, I prayed with my whole heart that the shame would force my parents to silently withdraw me from school without involving the principal. But, even as I prayed, I had little faith.

"As a prefect, you are supposed to be an example to the others. I didn't expect this from you, Ada," Mrs Oladokun, the principal of my school, Great Heights International College, continued addressing me.

My mother quietly nudged me from behind. I knew she wanted me to apologise, but I stood with my head bowed and did not utter a word.

Mrs Oladokun addressed my mother, saying, "I'm afraid, Mrs Ejiofor, we have rules and there are consequences for flouting them. You are an educator and so am I. You know the rules and I'm sure you abide by those rules in Aguda Grammar School. It's the same here; a pregnant girl can't continue schooling. There is nothing we can do. She will be expelled from our school."

It didn't come as a shock to either of us. We had expected it and my mother had come prepared.

"I agree that should be the right punishment, but she has registered for WAEC exams with this school already." My mother who had remained standing since we entered the principal's office then sat down, bringing her eyes to the same level with the principal's.

"She can return when WAEC starts and take her exams but she cannot continue schooling with us."

"That is what she wants - to hide from the shame at home - so this expulsion is very welcome by her. However, just like you, her father and I believe in consequences and have decided not to afford her the easy way out. She has to go through the shame of facing everyone and everything she knows. She should learn to deal with the result of her deeds, not run from them. This will serve as a deterrent to her sisters and to her as well in the future."

Mrs Oladokun blinked and the skin of her forehead creased. It was obvious she was having some kind of difficulty deciding. It was also easy to see she had been partially swayed by my mother's argument. I think my mother saw this and quickly dived in to pull down what was left of her defences.

"You can use her as an example to others. Tell them this is how they will be disgraced if they toe this line. Let them know they wouldn't be spared the shame. Let other girls who are tired of school and want to use this as the way out also be taught with this that getting pregnant is not a way out of growing up."

Mrs Oladokun, a small, wiry woman who wore small, square glasses that sat atop an aquiline nose and framed eyes that were permanently set in a scowl, was rarely flustered. If she was, she never let it show. But in that moment she was clearly confused. Her tiny lips, which rarely ever turned upwards or downwards, puckered as she considered.

"At least until she starts showing seriously, let her continue schooling here," my mother interrupted her thoughts.

Mrs Oladokun's eyeglasses came off at that point and she made a great show of wiping them. Despite sensing it was a lost cause, I sent up a desperate prayer that she would refuse to be swayed by mother's reasoning and send me home. However, she agreed.

"Ok. I will let her continue here but the moment her uniform can no longer hide the bulge she will have to stop. I don't want her bringing unnecessary attention to our prestigious school."

She returned the spectacles to her nose and hit her palm lightly on the desk, signalling that the meeting had come to an end.

"Your life is not over." My mother turned me around to face her as soon as we were out of the principal's office. "I will make sure of that. You hear?"

I nodded, though I wasn't convinced, and she seemed to sense my doubt because she put her hand to my chin and lifted my face till I was looking at her.

"This is not the end of the road for you," she said, stressing each word for emphasis. "If you play your cards right, this will be far from the end. Do you understand what I'm saying?"

"Yes mummy."

"Now, go to your class and carry on as always. I have to go back to school."

On the assembly ground the following morning, my insides were unsettled. The oversized sweater I wore to keep attention away from my still flat belly did nothing to keep the chill away. It seemed to be coming from inside my bones. I was certain the principal would bring me to the podium and I dreaded the moment when all the students would know what I had done. A wave of dizziness overtook me and instantly a pair of arms held me. Though my eyes were open, I could not see clearly and there was a ringing in my ear. I did not need the functioning of my senses to know whom the arms belonged to.

"Ama, I'm scared."

"Me too," she admitted in a shaky voice. "But we won't die."

"No, this is worse than death."

At the arrival of the principal, silence settled like a blanket over the assembly ground. Ama did not return to the line meant for her class, but stood behind me, giving support.

After the national and school anthems were recited, assembly proceeded as usual, with the teacher on duty conducting. I always considered the thirty minutes assembly too long, but as I waited to be called out and shamed, it seemed even longer. When it didn't happen just yet, I began to hope to be called already so I could be put out of my misery. Waiting was horrible.

Then it was time for the news and my name was called by the teacher on duty, not for my condition, but because, as the library prefect, it was my duty to read the news during every gathering. I had completely forgotten about the news and did not prepare for it.

Ama squeezed the arm she held from behind then I heard her say, "Kehinde, please hold Taiwo for me," before she went towards the podium.

Kehinde, as her name reveals, was born a twin too, but she lost her twin, Taiwo, when they were infants. When we came in as new students in J.S.S.1, Ama and I stuck together like we always did, letting no one into our very small circle. Kehinde tried to be, not just friends with us, but a part of that circle. Years of needing no one but each other meant we didn't know how to let anyone else in, even if we wanted to, but Kehinde kept at it.

Upon discovering we lived on the same street, it became even more impossible to avoid her. Once, when Ama was ill and didn't make it to school, since I was used to being part of a pair, I accepted Kehinde to be my companion for that day.

"Is your Taiwo in a different school?" I had asked only because I was expected to say something, not because I wanted to know.

"My Taiwo left me too early, when we were babies." She looked really sad, like it only happened recently. Afraid she was going to burst into tears, I quickly said the first thing I could think of to console her.

"I could be your Taiwo." Since then, I became a twin to two people. The name spread and some people started to call me "Ada Taiwo."

As Kehinde held on to me on the assembly ground, her concerned voice asking what was wrong, I was grateful to have another person I could lean on. I hoped she would always be there, just like Ama, even after she discovered my horrible mistake.

Taking charge, Ama had prepared the news and went on to read it to the students and teachers. Very few people could tell us apart and it seemed no one noticed, but Mrs. Oladokun did. As Ama folded the papers and was about to exit the podium, she stopped her. "Hold on, Ama."

A murmur rose among the students who finally realised the wrong twin had read the news.

"It is nice of you to take on from where your sister left off and ensure we have our news." Turning away from Ama, Mrs Oladokun looked in the direction of the line where S.S.3 students stood. She called for me to come up to the stage. I was grateful for Kehinde's support as she led me as far as she could to the wooden steps leading to the podium. With legs that shook, I climbed the steps and walked the rest of the way to join Mrs Oladokun.

Before revealing the details of my indiscretion to the school, she gave a long lecture.

"Akanjujaye oni jaye pe. Eni to ba farabale ni jaye pe," she said. Then for the benefit of those who did not understand the Yoruba language, she translated her words to English. "Be in a hurry to enjoy life and you wouldn't enjoy it for long. Take your time to enjoy life and you will enjoy it for a long time."

She continued: "Every rule we have laid down for you is not to punish you or to make your life miserable, but to guide you in the right path.

We, the adults, have been where you are now and know better to guide you through life. Unfortunately, some of you fail to adhere."

Reaching behind she pulled me forward. "Ada here, whom we all hold in high esteem, unfortunately, is one of those who failed to obey set rules and went ahead to disrespect herself and her body."

Total silence descended among the students. I could feel them holding their breaths, trying not to reach any conclusions. I also had the feeling that some had already drawn an inference from her statement about respect for self and the body.

Whenever I stood before the entire school during assembly to read the news, I consciously made efforts not to make eye contact with any of the students. Looking slightly above their heads, to the two-story block of classes behind them, kept me from faltering. It was a trick my mother had taught me the day I was made the library prefect. I had resolved to adopt the same approach to get through the ordeal, but for some unknown reason, I couldn't keep my eyes from searching those in the crowd.

"There is nothing done in the dark which does not come to light eventually. As I always tell you, you see this sun," she pointed and squinted towards the direction of the sun and, as though it were a completely novel object, the eyes of the students followed hers. "There is nothing hidden under it."

She paused, tapped the microphone, then delivered the words that changed my image in Great Heights International College forever.

"Ada has shamed herself, her family and this school by getting pregnant."

Loud exclamation rose from the students, drowning the principal's words. When the commotion continued, thereby making her speech impossible, the teachers went about trying to restore order.

What the eyes of my mates and juniors revealed reduced me to a pile of shame. I wanted to cease to exist. Shock, disbelief, gloating, condemnation, judgment, all these shone through their expressions, but the worst of all was the pity. It sent the message that there was nothing left to be envied and I was a disgrace. In a heartbeat, I moved from being a model student to being a disgrace.

Determined to prove that I still had some pride left, I swallowed the lump in my throat and opened my eyes wide to prevent the tears threatening to fall. Kehinde's mouth hanging open almost destroyed my efforts, but I held firm and dragged my gaze from the crowd's.

"How old are you?" Mrs Oladokun continued when silence returned once again. I knew I would cry if I spoke so I said nothing. This angered Mrs. Oladokun who turned on me with unrestrained fury.

"If you weren't pregnant I'd have ordered Mr. Wale to give you the beating of your life."

Every student dreaded being flogged by Mr. Wale, even the strongest boys. He flogged where it hurt the most and the least lashes he gave were twelve strokes.

"I am asking for the last time. How old are you?"

Ama rushed forward, "Fifteen ma. We are fifteen years old."

Shaking her head ruefully, she repeated, "Only fifteen. Pregnant at just fifteen." She turned to the rest of the school. "This is what happens when you misbehave; you destroy your future. I'm afraid Ada's life from now on will be dedicated to caring for a child. No more school or chasing dreams. Is that what you want for yourselves?"

"No!" they chorused loudly.

Three Fridays later, I attended my first antenatal appointment with my mother and Obinna, who made it back from school to be with me.

It came as no surprise that we were the youngest couple there and other expectant mothers looked at us curiously. Since the pregnancy was not showing yet, I hoped they would assume I came with my mother, but the more observant ones, who knew all the signs and did not need a round stomach to tell them what was going on beneath the surface, looked at me with judgment in their eyes. So did the nurses who got me registered.

The doctor was not quick to mask his surprise at our presence when Obinna and I got into his office. At this point, Obinna, who had had enough of the silent criticism from everyone, snapped.

"She's pregnant, not dying. Is she the youngest pregnant person you've ever seen?"

Adjusting his eyeglasses, I expected the doctor to take offence, but he didn't. He gave a benign smile and motioned for us to sit. "Actually I have seen younger people, but in this particular hospital you are the youngest. Am I right to assume you are responsible for the pregnancy?"

"Well, at least she didn't have an abortion. We are doing the right thing," Obinna said defensively, ignoring the doctor's question.

"Which is the thing I'll like to talk to you about." With his elbows on his desk, he steepled his hands and looked from me to Obinna and back. He cleared his throat, giving the impression that he was going to say something serious. I steeled myself for it.

He began, "Sometimes the *right* thing is relative. Keeping a baby isn't always the right thing if you won't give it all the care it deserves or if it poses a risk to your life." He paused for his words to sink in.

Having expected to hear something graver, I exhaled. Along with my relief came a sliver of hope sown by the doctor's words. The thought that I did not have to go through with the pregnancy, that I could choose not to be subjected to the bleak future everyone foresaw for me, was liberating. Before I could give the thought further consideration, the Catholic teachings instilled in me since I was a little girl attending Catechism classes rose to the surface and clamped down on the thought with such finality, leaving me scandalized.

"Are you suggesting we abort this, doctor?" Obinna's voice had gone up several octaves.

"I am not suggesting that. I am simply letting you know that you have options."

"We will not have an abortion," I said. I was tired and couldn't even afford to exhibit Obinna's indignation.

"Religious reasons? What church do you attend?" The doctor wanted to know.

"It's not about church…" Obinna's eyes shot to the name tag on the table "…Doctor Mark, please just do whatever you can do to see that she can have a safe pregnancy and let us worry about the rest."

In that moment, I noticed how much Obinna had changed suddenly; how fearless, mature and in control he seemed.

Doctor Mark nodded and shuffled through pamphlets on his desk. When he found what he was looking for, he handed us one pamphlet each. It had the picture of a smiling biracial woman holding a happy biracial baby in the air. The moment I realized it was an advertisement for an adoption service, I felt dizzy and dropped the leaflet.

"Nope, we're not interested," Obinna said, shaking his head vigorously.

The doctor ignored him and looked pointedly at me, waiting for my answer.

The thought of giving my baby away made me feel a sense of loss. Mrs Oladokun's words replayed in my mind.

"I'm afraid Ada's life from now on will be dedicated to caring for a child. No more school or chasing dreams."

The loss I felt when Mrs Oladokun said those words seemed inconsequential when compared to the ache in my chest at the thought of giving my child to someone else. I realized then that if I had to choose between giving up my child or giving up my dreams, I would choose the latter.

"No, doctor," I answered with conviction. "I'm not giving my child up for adoption.

"OK. Now that we have that out of the way…" he looked at the open file in front of him and back at me, "It says here that you're 15?"

I nodded.

He turned his gaze to Obinna and asked, "How old are you?"

Obinna hesitated and wouldn't meet the doctor's eyes.

"Are you up to 18?" Doctor Mark said.

"No sir," Obinna said simply.

The doctor sighed softly, leaned forward and regarded me with sympathy in his eyes. When he spoke, I could also sense sympathy in his words. "I will like to meet with your parent or a guardian who is of age. Can you arrange that?"

I nodded. "My mum, she's seeing a doctor in the other room. She'll join us when she's done."

"Good." Standing, Doctor Mark motioned for me to move to the bed in a corner of his office. The mackintosh bed cover was uncomfortable and stuck to my skin as I obeyed.

"Close this place, please," I requested when he didn't bother to pull the partitioning in place. I saw the hurt in Obinna's eyes before the partition was adjusted, blocking him out.

There was no time to dwell on how I made him feel or anything else because, soon, my body began taking more assault than I cared to handle.

He started with questions which I answered as calmly as possible. Most, I did not have answers to, especially the questions about my family history and the date when I last saw my period. I never kept count. Just when I thought the entire visit would involve answering questions alone, he gestured for me to lie down and began to prod and feel. His touch felt too intimate. The closest I had ever been with anyone else physically was the evening the baby growing inside me was conceived. My thought travelled back to that rainy day in November and my heart thudded fast at the memory. A lone tear slid down my temple into my hair. I realized that an unrepentant part of me did not regret my actions, I only regretted the outcome.

"Do you feel any pain?" Doctor Mark asked upon noticing the tear and I shook my head. He reached on the table beside the bed for something remotely resembling an intercom, which I later came to know as the Sonicaid, applied gel on my belly and began to probe. He listened for a while then frowned.

"I think you should have an ultrasound soonest."

Having complications had never occurred to me, but at his grave tone and look, it did, causing me to tense up.

"Is everything OK, doctor?" I heard the panic in my voice. Almost immediately Obinna pushed the partition aside a little, looked in, then nudged the barrier out of the way completely and joined us. Concern was etched in his features.

Mother rapped twice on the door, opened it slightly, then rushed in when she saw the look on our faces.

"I'm her mother. Is everything OK, doctor?"

"As far as I can tell everything seems fine," he began, but we were still unconvinced and I was about to ask the reason for his reaction when he spoke again. "However, I can hear more than one heartbeat. From my experience, it's most likely you are expecting more than one child."

"No!" I objected loudly, like my refusal could change things. Obinna sat heavily on the bed, his rear brushing against my feet. Mother moved to the head of the bed and held my hand.

"We will only be certain with the result of the ultrasound, but I am almost sure you will be having twin babies. However, even if the scan reveals what I already believe, there is always the possibility of the vanishing twin syndrome, so we will have to have another scan when your pregnancy advances to reach an accurate conclusion."

"Don't begin to worry just yet," he hastened to add.

I had stopped paying attention at the mention of *twin babies*. I never wanted a child so soon and there I was carrying two. I wanted to howl at the injustice of it all. Why should just one mistake get me in this condition while people who have been sexually active for years walk free? There were so many women looking for just one child for years and here I was about to have two that I was not ready for.

The gravity of my situation hit me with such force that my breath came in quick gasps. My life as I knew it had changed forever.

Chapter Four

Upon discovering I was to be a father, not to one but two babies, I realised I couldn't be the same person I had always been.

The news filled me with conflicting emotions. There was the fear, a little bit of regret, uncertainty, even a longing to go back and change things. But there was also pride. I decided then never to admit it to anyone, but the feeling was unmistakable. I was about to have something that was mine; creatures who will be solely dependent on me for everything and I resolved to make sure I became very dependable. I was going to prove everyone wrong.

I felt a certain urgency to begin creating and living the life I had always had in a part of my imagination tagged as 'future'. My future wasn't tomorrow or next year anymore. It had begun. To start with, I had to make things right with you and reassure you. That was why I came. It hadn't been my intention to start trouble. If anything, I was trying to avoid it at all cost.

I folded the paper in my hand and looked up into Ama's face. She had not bothered to sit after delivering the letter from Obinna. The mild rebuke evident on her face communicated better than words what she thought of my action towards Obinna when he stopped by the house earlier.

My parents were not home. Immediately we returned from Mass, they had lunch and left for the monthly meeting of our people, the Isuofia Indigenes, in Lagos. I had begun to avoid coming out to the parlour whenever my parents were around and, as a result, I had missed watching television. The one in our room had stopped working and I did not feel I had a right to ask my parents for anything at all, much less to repair the television. *Edge of Paradise*, my favourite television show on Sundays, was to come on in a few minutes. Since my parents were away, I was on my way to the parlour to watch my show when Obinna's voice stopped me while I was still in the hallway.

Through the open door of the hallway, I watched Nnenna, who had let Obinna in, walk him to a chair.

"Obidaddy…" she greeted him in her unique way and knelt on the far end of the same couch Obinna was seated on.

"Nnedaddy," he replied, replacing the "nna" in her name with its English equivalent "daddy."

"Your wife is sleeping. You want me to wake her?" Nnenna's smile was mischievous just like everything else about her.

"No, don't disturb her. And she is not my wife." The smile forming on Obinna's face froze when suddenly Nnenna jumped off the chair, her face a picture of disdain.

"What? So you are planning to dump my sister?" She screamed at the top of her lungs. He raised both palms to calm her, but her shout grew louder.

"So you get my sister pregnant and just want to leave her? You are just evil." She glowered then turned on her heels and ran inside, almost bumping into me in the dark hallway. The commotion brought Ama out from the kitchen.

Staring confused after the receding figure of Nnenna, Ama asked amid a yawn, "What is that?"

Obinna stammered through his explanation. Ama shook her head repeatedly then sat on the table at the centre of the parlour and faced him.

"You shouldn't have told her that. Everyone is worried you'll leave Ada one day and move on with your life, while she's stuck at this level all her life. You are young. Anything can happen. Nnenna is just very worried for Ada right now. You know how she has always looked up to her."

"I just didn't mean it that way." He blew out an exaggerated breath, rubbed his face with both hands, let them fall to his side then leaned back, his head against the head rest. I chose that time to make myself visible.

I felt sore all over and gingerly settled into the seat beside Obinna. This brought me face to face with my reflection on the glass cabinet housing the television and video player. I thought I looked fragile and pale and that ate into my confidence. Ama exited quietly.

"Are you in pain?" Obinna asked suddenly, concern creasing his forehead.

"Why does everyone keep asking me that? I'm pregnant, not sick." My words came out sounding angrier than I meant for it to.

"Have I done something wrong?"

Rather than answer his query, I arched my eyebrows, looking at him intently.

He explained further: "I feel your parents are acting differently towards me but that's understandable, then Nnenna just went off on me. Ama seems irritated as well."

"You are just being paranoid Obinna." I dismissed his concerns with a wave of my hand then put the same hand to my forehead and sighed. I could feel the beginning of a headache.

"Are you sure you are OK?"

"I am fine!" My outburst took me by surprise. "Or maybe I'm not. Who in my condition will be? I am the one who will have to put my life on hold to take care of kids, the one who will have to give up on my aspirations and be subjected to a bleak future. How can I be all right?"

He started to answer but I lifted my hand, cutting him off. "I don't expect an answer from you. You have your entire life before you. After the kids are born and you have assuaged your conscience and done all you feel is right by them you'll move on and have a full life, get a job, get married and be all you want." I stabbed a finger against his knee viciously. "I am the one whose life has stopped!" I was breathing fast. My chest heaved painfully like my heart was about to burst out of it. Feeling spent, I leaned forward, resting my face in both palms and concentrated on breathing slowly.

After a long while, during which I felt in control again, I turned to Obinna, hoping he would take the cue and leave. I was afraid and having voiced those fears I felt ashamed and wanted to be left alone.

"Ada, I came here to talk to you about my plans for our future." His voice sounded hesitant, unsure whether to speak or remain silent.

"I don't need you planning my future."

"No, I know you can do that on your own, but it's obvious to me you think I will just move on and leave you to handle things on your own. I want you to know we are in this together and I'm never leaving you."

I scoffed. "People move on, meet new people, feelings change, you are in school after all, where there are many fine girls. Anything could happen. I won't blame you, though."

He cupped my chin and tried to guide my eyes to his. I wondered what he was expecting me to see there. I sensed the sincerity in his words, seeing it in his eyes would lead me to believe anything he says and because I didn't want that, I kept my eyes averted.

"I plan to get a job."

That got my attention. "And stop school?"

"No. I will combine both." He explained his plans to me about schooling, working, and settling down with me eventually. Hope and doubt warred as I imagined the life he painted vividly with his words. I wanted that life, but I was not naïve to trust in it.

He left when he saw I wouldn't be convinced, then sent a letter through Ama. His letter was as convincing as his words were but I knew better than to be hopeful.

Words are easily formed, intentions are mostly well meaning, but action is always the determinant. I thought as I read through his letter again that I would have to wait for the future to find out how things turn out.

Chapter Five

It was 2004 and Nigeria was on the brink of a technological revolution. With the influx of mobile phones and affordable personal computers into the Nigerian market, access to the internet became easier. It was in view of this that Obinna decided to tap into this growing industry. Though studying Architecture at the University, he told me he planned to secure a job as an intern with an ICT firm.

His new schedule of attending classes by day, job hunting in the evenings and visiting home every weekend to be with me must have been hard for him to handle. The effort he made was not lost on me and I was grateful and began to believe that brighter days lay ahead.

That year was the toughest I ever lived through. By the third week of February, nineteen weeks into my pregnancy, I sat for my JAMB examination and when the second term of school ended for the Easter break in April, I knew I would not be returning for the third term. My tummy was growing bigger every day.

School was not the only place I was denied access to. I was excommunicated from the church choir and that meant I could not participate fully in the Easter festivities. The solemn songs of Lent and the victorious hymns of Easter, I listened to wistfully, sitting at Mass with every other parishioner, rather than at the exalted position reserved for choristers.

As I prepared for the WAEC examination, I grew heavier and more fatigued. During the day, the lesson teachers employed to coach me at home prepared me for the forthcoming exams. Ama and I scheduled the night time for our reading sessions, though I could barely ever keep my eyes open and woke up most mornings with my books serving as a pillow.

I also continued to attend my prenatal check-ups with my mother until she gave birth one early morning in June. That same day, I sat for my Math exam and looked forward to my delivery date; the day I would regain freedom from the incessant back pain, nausea, and curious stares from people wondering why such a small girl had such big stomach.

That day eventually arrived in the last week of August. It was a stormy day, reminiscent of the weather the day the babies were conceived.

It had been sunny for most of the week prior to the birth, but that morning it changed suddenly. As my water broke, the rain fell in heavy unremitting drops, giving me the feeling that it was God scolding me for my indiscretion.

After the birth, I came to realize that carrying and birthing a child was the easy part. The real test of character comes from the frequent sleepless nights and having to attend to totally helpless creatures relying on you for their every need. It did not help how fragile they were, or the thought that every single action taken from the day they were born would somehow mould and have a lasting effect on them.

Lots of changes happened after I had my kids. I had always seen my mother as the perfect, infallible, all-knowing one, who never made mistakes and knew what to do in every situation. When I became aware of my pregnant state, I knew I had to change in every way into a maternal figure, and I tried. Yet, once in a while I lapsed into being a child again. However, the moment I beheld my children, a boy and a girl, there was a sort of psychological shift, so palpable, I felt the exact moment I went from one phase to another; from dependent to dependable. I knew these beings, hardly bigger than a foot, were relying on me to be the perfect mother for them. I decided to be just that.

It started with giving up my sleep. I loved to sleep. Usually, when we had to go to school, Ama would be dressed and having breakfast before I jumped out of bed to get ready. I never thought it possible that I would get used to getting by on very little sleep, but I had developed a sensibility for the wellbeing of the kids and would check up on them up to five times a night, the way my mother always checked up on us.

The twins shared a room with my baby brother Chukwuemeka and, almost always, while I was doing the nightly rounds, my mother would be doing same, so that we ended up walking into each other in the children's room most nights.

We bonded over this night-time routine. Our relationship moved beyond mother and daughter to a kind of sisterhood. We became friends and there was a growing respect for each other. I respected her more because of the fortitude she had to go through this for all seven of us. On her part, I sensed her respect for me grew because of how I rose to my new responsibility. She commended me on that once.

The older they grew the greater their needs, so much so that I began to wonder if I would still be able to make it into the university that year as planned.

While we watched our kids sleep one night my mother broached the subject.

"You know your result is out, o kwa ya?"

I nodded.

"You don't seem eager to check it."

"What's the hurry? Ama will check for me when she's checking hers." Truth be told I was afraid to check it. I had passed JAMB, barely exceeding the cut-off mark, and was even less confident about the WAEC result.

"The only reason Ama hasn't checked hers is because of you. She is trying not to rush you and is waiting for you to indicate that you are ready," she pointed out sympathetically.

Mother understood us all in a way no one ever did and that made it easy for me to open up to her.

"How will I combine this," I gestured to the kids, "and my education? I hear University is even more demanding than secondary school."

Mother smiled knowingly then sat on the rocking chair. I lowered my tired body to the floor beside her and looked around the room that was formerly used as the guest bedroom. The four walls were painted in different colours; blue, green, yellow and orange. The rug covering most of the room was also in the same rich, vibrant colours. For a moment it occurred to me, like it usually did, that there was no pink colour anywhere in the room as was traditional for baby girls. Perhaps that was why I compensated by using mostly pink clothes for my daughter. Even now, nestled beside her brother, she was dressed in baby pink overalls.

Against one wall, there were two wooden cots; Chukwuemeka lay in one while Chika and Chuka lay together in the bigger cot made to fit two babies. Each baby was covered with a miniature mosquito net. The fan standing between the cots and the dresser, which was always turned on the lowest, blew cool breeze across my cheek and threatened to dislodge my loose-fitting hairnet. I found that this room always gave me some measure of peace.

"Your situation is no different from mine," mother stated finally. "I was a student when I was pregnant with you and your sister."

"But married," I pointed out.

"Marriage doesn't make it any easier. If anything, it made it tougher. I had a husband to care for, a home to keep and children." She rubbed her tummy now and her eyes took on a faraway look, like she was reliving it all.

"Most of my pre-degree courses were taken on my knees because the chairs were too close to the table and could not accommodate my growing stomach. One time I almost fainted on campus because of the stress. Then you two came along and so did my exams. I stayed up most nights, both of you in each arm and a book which I tried to read on my lap, but you didn't make it easy for me. You in particular. You were very active and would reach for my books. You succeeded in tearing most of them."

I shook my head in denial.

"Eziokwu. It is true. I particularly remember one night. It was two a.m. and I had an exam by nine in the morning. I hadn't slept at all and

I had not gone beyond a few pages in my book, then you two began crying, at the same time o. I did everything to get you to sleep, but nothing worked. Hmmm. As dawn neared, I flung my books on the floor, dropped you crying babies on the bed and joined you in crying. My cry was so loud that you stopped in shock, then you carried on crying until we all fell asleep."

I laughed. She laughed too.

"Trust me, your children are being merciful to you. I wasn't that lucky with you. At a time I decided to give up on going to the university. Most women at the time who were married didn't feel the need for a university education, but my mother wouldn't hear of it."

"'There is dignity is making your own money,' she would always say. 'Go to the university, get a good job and earn respect for yourself. Your dreams do not end because you have a family.' Now I am saying the same to you." With great effort, she stood from the chair. I stood too and positioned myself in front of her to block her exit from the room.

"But it is too hard. Maybe I should wait till next year." My eyes pleaded for understanding.

"Mbelede nyiri dike, mana mbelede k'eji ama dike." She delivered an Igbo proverb then laughed at my confused look. "All you township children sef. What I'm trying to say is that it is during times of adversity that we know who is really strong. Don't shy away from tough situations, they make you tougher." She put a hand to my chin and looked me in the eye meaningfully before leaving the room.

In the morning I gave Ama the go-ahead to check my result.

"If I did well, just call home straight from the cyber café and end this tension. If I didn't, don't tell me anything about the result," I told Ama as she was leaving the house to check our WAEC result.

"You will do well, don't worry."

When she left, I could not be still. I paced and had to empty my bladder multiple times. My eyes kept straying to the clock and each time it showed that time had barely passed since she left, yet it felt like she had been gone for too long. When I could not take it anymore, I went outside the gate of our compound and stood, looking down the street for any sign of her, then I went back inside, hoping the land phone would ring and it would be Ama.

She returned about an hour later wearing a sombre look. One look at her face and I thought I knew my fate. I refused the printed result sheet she passed to me.

"I told you I don't want to see it. How is yours?" I asked, trying not to be self-centred.

"Why don't you open it first now?"

Nnenna came out then, grabbed the sheet from Ama's hand, almost tearing it in the process and opened it. Her eyes shot up and she looked at me, a smile playing across her lips. Out of curiosity I snatched the paper from her hand, skimmed through in a hurry, then, not believing my eyes, went back up and began looking at each grade more carefully. I dropped to the floor and laughed breathlessly in relief. Ama laughed too.

"Elaa! I got you!"

"How dare you scare me like this?"

"University here we come!" She gave an ecstatic whoop and hugged me tightly. The rest of my sisters; Ujunwa, Olanma and Ifeyichi, came out to see what the excitement was about and soon joined in too. Even Ifeyichi who was too young to understand the seriousness of a WAEC examination, or a university education for that matter, was bouncing around in excitement.

For the rest of that day I was in high spirits. Everything made me smile in a way I had not done in a while, even the twins' bawling made me smile.

Father's return was the acme. When Ama showed him the result, he regarded me with an expression I had ceased to see in his eyes since he became aware of my pregnancy.

"I didn't think you could pull this off, but you did. You have made me proud. Both of you," he said to include Ama. "Let's hope this is a sign of better things to come. And now, I think two of you are ready for your own GSM phones."

Ama and I looked at each other and squealed in delight, not minding that it was late at night or that the babies were sleeping, and we were rewarded with an answering squeal that did not sound delightful in any way from all three babies. Laughing, mother, Ama and I hurried to their room and carried each child, soothing them back to sleep.

Chapter Six

As the year was winding down and a new academic year began, I waited patiently to receive news that I had been admitted into the university. Ama had been admitted based on merit. Her result was deserving of the honour and she had already resumed school. She was going from home, agreeing only to become a boarder when I join her in university.

Upon her return each day, she regaled me with stories about school, her exciting anecdotes taking me through an institution I had never been to and revealing to me vivid mental pictures of what it would be like. I was already living the university life through her, but wanted to experience it for myself. As the new experiences she shared with me increased, so did my impatience.

One evening, she returned home with bad news. The penultimate admission list was released that morning and my name still was not there. Desperation can make us do things we never thought ourselves capable of. It had me awake that night considering various courses of action. By morning I had not slept at all, but my mind was clear and decided.

Not long after my sisters left for school, I got ready to execute the decision I had arrived at the night before. Though fully dressed and set to go, I paced around in my room, listening to the sounds made by my mother in the parlour and waiting to see if she would go into another room so I could leave without having to explain my movement.

Chukwuemeka was down with fever, so she took the day off to tend to him. When it became apparent that she did not plan on leaving anytime soon, I resolved to brave it out.

In the parlour, mother was rocking a fretful Chukwuemeka with one arm and trying to hold steady a paper on which was written a medicine description with the other hand. Her head shot up before I could sneak out.

"Where are you going?" She eyed the white blazer I was wearing on top of a black gown and black shoes to match.

"Just to the cyber café to print out my JAMB result slip. I only checked it the first time, but I was not with enough money to print it out," I lied.

"Must you do it now? Why not wait for Nnenna or Ujunwa to come back from school and help you with it?"

"Mummy I won't be long." I quickly hurried towards the door before she could come up with a genuine reason to stop me. She did stop me before I made it out of the house.

"Is it just to go to the cyber café here that you are wearing shoe and carrying handbag?"

I mumbled incoherently and quickly made it through the door.

The gate of UNILAG was just exactly as Ama had described it, every part of it, such that I began to feel a sense of deja vu. It felt like coming home. It was not my first time in the school. I had been there when I was an infant, safely strapped to my mother's back while she moved from one lecture hall to another. Emotions welled up at the thought that I started out here, even before I knew what a school meant, and would want to complete my education here. This strengthened my resolve to pull through with what had brought me to the University. Having stepped through the gates, I knew no other University would do for me.

Not wanting to expose myself as a novice, I ignored the instinct to ask for directions to the Social Science faculty, and instead made my way down the walkway, branching off into every building, looking at the sign in front of each to deduce which department it was. After passing so many buildings without finding the right one, I gave in and asked an old man in work overalls to point me in the right direction. Several minutes later, during which I missed my way and asked for directions again, I made it to my destination.

It had Faculty of Social Sciences written boldly on the sign board placed in front of the block. Taking a deep breath to steady my heart, which was thumping wildly I feared people could hear it, I walked into the building and intuitively searched for the Economics department.

I found it to the right of the corridor on the first floor and pushed open the door after saying a quick, silent prayer. An unsmiling female looked up quizzically, her eyes asking all the questions without the help of her mouth. The old me, the person I was before being a mother, would have been tempted to cower, but since having the twins I had become fearless. I had done the worst and had heard the worst being said about me. I felt there was nothing else to fear, with this in mind I closed the door behind me and approached her desk.

She looked like the type who could be intimidating but who could also be easily intimidated by very confident people who knew their place. Deciding then it would do no good to reveal how uncertain I was, I squared my shoulders, looked her straight in the eyes and deepened my voice to make me sound more confident.

"I am here to see Professor Okoro." I said the name like I was familiar with him and was pleased to see her calm and aloof disposition falter a bit.

"Do you have an appointment?" The confusion on her face was visible. She was obviously unsure whether to treat me like an important visitor or like a pesky fly. Her face showed her struggle between both. I was determined to press the advantage I already had and keep up my confident stance even though my toes curled and uncurled stiffly in my shoes.

"I didn't get a chance to book one, but if you can fix me in somewhere today I will appreciate it."

"Is he expecting you?"

"No, he is not. Is he in?" I added quickly, seeing the frown return to her forehead.

"He is not around."

"I will wait then. Can I sit?" I indicated the couch at a corner of the office and she reluctantly nodded her acquiescence.

I busied myself going over in my mind the speech I had prepared the night before. Ama's stories had not been restricted to the school structures alone, but also encompassed some lecturers and students worth mentioning. Professor Okoro, was one of those lecturers who one never left the school without having heard of, whether you were his student or not. Those who have the misfortune of being his students could not wait to graduate, some wished for him to die while others hoped for his retirement, and those who had no reason to take his class thanked God for the lucky escape. He was the most dreaded lecturer and everyone, both within and outside his faculty, spoke about him.

"No matter how good a student you are, the best you can get in my course is a C. A is for God and since no student can be that excellent then no one deserves an A. B is only for those as good as I am. I am certain none of you have attained the level of Professor hence none of you can claim to know enough to deserve a B. I give each what he deserves and if you work hard enough you get a C. If not, well there is always an opportunity to carry over. That's the beauty of life, there are always second chances and in some cases even third, and fourth chances as have been seen in this department."

That is the famous induction speech he delivers to each new class of students every year. Ama was not his student and she was extremely grateful for that, but she had been to my faculty enough times and had gleaned enough information about my department of choice and the lecturers who would be teaching me. She had even made friends with some students in the Economics department on my behalf and booked their notes in advance for when I finally got in.

I was terrified to meet Professor Okoro, but more than that, I was afraid to wait one extra year at home and that fear overshadowed the former so that I remained in my position, rather than slip through the doors like I wanted to when it opened and admitted a towering man with deep lines between his brows and around his eyes, presenting his face in an intimidating frown.

He ignored the greeting from the lady at the desk, his long legs eating up the distance leading to the door of his office in three strides, then stopped abruptly at my voice. His hand paused on the door knob and his head turned toward me.

I stood quickly before his head completed its rotation to settle on my face. The lines between his brows deepened further. His scowl was frightening to the extent that my bladder threatened to embarrass me.

"Good morning, sir."

I was still aware enough to register that my voice was firm and did not shake. That surprised me. Apparently, it surprised him too.

He turned toward me fully, his face mirroring the puzzlement I had seen earlier on that of his secretary. He was not sure what to make of me. I could almost tell no one had stood before him and sounded that bold. Ignoring my quivering nerves and full bladder, I decided I had nothing to lose. Silently, I asked myself the question Ama and I usually asked each other in desperate situations. *What's the worst that could happen?*

I would probably get thrown out of his office, but I was not his student – yet - so there was no threat of being marked down in his course or of my result being withheld. The thought emboldened me.

Balancing the books he held in the crook of his left arm he stood ramrod straight. "Who are you?"

His voice was even more threatening and this made me forget the speech I had rehearsed. It felt as though a mound was stuck in my throat.

"I am nobody sir, nobody worth your attention, but with your help I can be somebody," I said

He was a proud man I could tell, one who likes to feel important. My words fulfilled that need in him, but I knew I should not overdo it lest he begins to feel too powerful and sees me as less than worthy of his attention.

"Can I see you in your office, sir?" I heard a quick intake of breath and turned to find his secretary looking at me shocked. *The audacity!* I read in her expression. I expected Mr Okoro to feel the same way and was half anticipating the next words out of his mouth to be a rebuke.

"Abike, inform me as soon as Professor Akinolu arrives," he said instead and opened the door to his office. Without waiting for a reply from his secretary, he ushered me in.

His office was just as one would expect of a man like him: no personal photographs, no bright colours, just a shelf filled with hard covered, large-volume books. The top of the shelf held award plaques of various materials and sizes. His desk was empty save for a desktop computer. Rounding his desk, he opened a drawer and slid the books he carried into it before sitting. He did not invite me to take a seat. With fingers intertwined, he looked at me for a very long time through wide eyes, until I was tempted to squirm. I decided to fill in the silence.

"Sir, I am Ada. Ada Ejiofor. I passed both my JAMB and WAEC exams in one sitting. Unfortunately, my name has not been in any of the lists released. This admission means everything to me." The words rushed out and when I was done he kept looking at me, saying nothing. The puzzle was gone from his face and impatience was fast taking its place.

"Sir, look my results are ok." I brought my documents out from my bag and held them towards him. He did not move a muscle neither did he look at the papers. He simply kept his eyes fixed on mine, his gaze hardening with each second. I wondered what to do next to get through to him.

"I promise to be the best student I can be if you help me get in." I still was not getting through to him. It was obvious it did not matter to him whether I chose to be the best student or not.

I decided to try another route. I would crawl if need be.

"Please give me this chance sir. You have no idea the impact you will be making in my life if you do."

I knelt at that point, my head barely visible above his desk. "Please sir, I took my future into my hands and risked your wrath to come here. I considered you may not approve of my coming to you, yet I took the risk. Now my future is in your hands. You are the only hope I have now."

There was nothing more to say so I held my breath and waited. Relief coursed through me when his expression softened slightly. He leaned forward and gestured for me to stand. I did but still did not sit.

He took a deep breath, released it slowly. Pursing his lips, he cast his eyes around then let them settle on me again.

"I know it's not up to you, sir," I added quickly, sensing it was what he was about to say. "But you wield such great influence in this school. I'm certain if anyone can make this happen it is you."

His lips stretched in what I figured to be his way of smiling. It was obvious he rarely did that. His face appeared strained with the effort. "You'll make a formidable negotiator."

I smiled not knowing what else to do.

"I will see what I can do."

He stood then and moved toward the large shelf occupying most of the space in the room. I turned my head to follow his movement. On the floor beside the shelf lay a package. He tore the white paper wrapper to reveal textbooks. He retrieved the one on top and held it out to me. I collected it.

"A new list will be pasted next Monday and if your result is as good as you say, I'll do what I can to see that your name will be on it," he said as he stretched out his hand to collect the photocopies of my WAEC and JAMB result.

The taste of triumph is empowering. I tasted it then, not in my tongue, no, it started from my head coursing through my veins and flowed through every part of my body down to my feet, filling my stomach and energizing me. The hunger I had registered feeling earlier and ignored was quenched completely and strength surged through me. I wanted to jump, dance, run, hug Prof. Okoro, anything at all, but I settled for a slight bow and a profusion of *Thank you, sir,* showering him with more blessings than I had offered any single human being at a time.

I made for the door, impatient to share the news with my family, but he stopped me.

"Don't think that textbook is for free. As soon as you resume bring one thousand five hundred naira. That's how much it costs."

I looked at the slim volume in my hand. Introduction to basic Economics by J.N Okoro. It shouldn't be more than four hundred naira, I thought, but what did it matter. "No problem sir. I will."

"And you better begin studying. There is a quiz in less than 2 weeks. You'll need to work hard to earn your C. I don't like dull students."

"I'll work hard for an A sir," I said, testing him.

His countenance reverted to the one I had first seen when I came in, the scowl returning. "You might be smart but not that smart. See you next week."

As I journeyed home, I channelled the excess energy my excitement had generated into rebuking all the death wishes students of many sets had made upon Professor Okoro's life and prayed God to preserve him, at least until the following week.

I came home to loud wails. From the gate leading into the compound, I could hear them as I jogged into the house.

"Where have you been?" Mother's eyes went to the clock. She rocked two babies in the crook of each arm and one strapped to her back. My eyes followed hers. 2:15 P.M.

I hurried to her and took one child from her arm and was already sitting and unzipping my dress to nurse the child when I realized it was Chukwuemeka. I returned him and took Chika.

"I went to school to work my admission."

She gave me a slanted look from up to down and back again, her lips pursed all the while. "Work kwa? What nonsense are you saying?"

I recounted everything that had happened and when I was done she opened her mouth, closed it almost immediately and simply stood regarding me with what I interpreted as wonderment in her eyes.

When the babies were all pacified and home was quiet again, I found that I was still restless. Several times I held my phone and started dialling Ama's number then, deciding it would be more satisfactory to see the expression on her face when I told her, I held myself back.

Hours passed and I finally gave up trying to come up with an activity to exhaust me so that I could keep still. I desperately needed an outlet. In the past, when I needed to open up to anyone, it was always with Ama, but when she was unavailable the next option would be Kehinde.

I thought of her then and wondered if it would be a good idea to visit her. Though we lived on the same street, it had been a month since I last saw her and even longer before that. It wasn't always that way. We saw every day when school was in session and during the holidays the longest we stayed before visiting each other was two days. Circumstances had taken its toll on our friendship, a friendship I tried desperately to save, but gave up on after visiting her at home several times only to be informed that she was not home, even though I could hear the hum of the sewing machine coming out of her room as she engaged in the only hobby she allowed herself have outside of her numerous books; a hobby we thought odd for a girl our age, yet benefitted from every time we had spare Ankara material that we needed to use or a dress that needed mending.

Her mother would stand by the door separating the parlour from the rooms, her large body taking a stance that dared me to look inside or try to go further, yet smiling sweetly and enquiring about my parents and how I was coping. Rejection I could take, but not disrespect. When Idowu and Bode, Kehinde's younger ones, would come into their parlour, see me and refuse to acknowledge my presence or greet, I did not need anyone to tell me I was no longer welcome there.

If it was hard on me, I assumed it was harder on Kehinde. Whenever we bumped into each other, she would look at me with guilt and apology in her eyes and when I tried to engage in a conversation I would see her constantly looking around uncomfortably.

In spite of all that had happened, I wanted to see her badly, not just for the friendship we shared, but to let her see what I had accomplished. More than that, I hoped her family would also be around to hear what I had to share. Maybe then they would see that I am not a useless child, I thought.

"Where are you going to this time; to see the Vice Chancellor?"

I chuckled at mother's question.

"So I am now a desperado that will be calling on all university super powers? I'm going to see Kehinde."

Her brows came together at this and she was silent for some seconds. When she spoke it was with some measure of caution.

"I know you want to go and tell them about your admission. Must you? Why not wait till your name comes out?" She lifted both shoulders and snapped the fingers of both hands at me. I thought she would try to dissuade me using her authority as the parent. "Personally, I feel you should not go at all. They've made it clear they don't want you there, so why go?"

With any other person, I would not have divulged my real reason for going but it was different with mother.

"Maybe because I want to show them that something good can still come out of me."

"You don't need to prove anything. Let your achievements speak for you."

"My achievement will speak for me through my own mouth. Mummy I am going to see her."

"You never listen. Make sure you come back early. I don't think I can handle them alone when they wake up."

In less than ten minutes I was standing in front of the compound that had once been like home to me. I always thought it would have been a very beautiful house if the words *"This house is not for sell. Thank you. Try bush"* were not splayed in large red paint across the front of the building. The fact that whoever wrote the words spelt *sell* instead of *sale* did not help matters. I often teased Kehinde that anyone passing by would get the impression that illiterates, and not people as sophisticated as her family, lived in the house. She explained that those words had been painted on that wall even before she was born. Her father had inherited it from his father and was a man who attached value to things that had emotional significance. This made it hard for him to modify most of his inheritance, except those that were absolutely necessary.

At the door, I lifted the ring of the antique brass door knocker fashioned in the shape of a lion's head and rapped the door twice with it then moved slightly to the side to avoid being seen through the peephole. I could not risk being turned back.

"Who is it?" Kehinde's voice asked just on the other side of the door.

"Taiwo."

"Taiwo? Which Taiwo?" She sounded suspicious.

"Kehinde, it's me, Ada."

Silence, then urgent murmurs followed. After some seconds, longer than expected for one standing just by the door to open, the door was eased open slightly to reveal Kehinde, with her body blocking the entrance.

"Sorry, the key was not in the key hole," she supplied guiltily, looking a few inches to my right. Her eyes would not meet mine.

"Am I allowed to come in?" It was funny to me that I had to ask that question considering how I used to barge in, sometimes without bothering to knock. She hesitated then opened the door reluctantly. Her body still covered most of the entrance so I eased in through the small space between her and the wall.

I entered their parlour to meet two pairs of eyes trained on me. They were filled with suspicion and curiosity; in that peculiar way one would regard a stranger.

"Good afternoon aunty and uncle." I bowed in mock courtesy and was relieved to notice their discomfort. At least they still had some sense to recognise the error in their attitude towards me.

"Oh, sorry. Good afternoon," Bode corrected his misbehaviour.

"Good afternoon. Sorry. It's just that we were not expecting you," Idowu paraphrased.

I was familiar with the house in a way that I could tell if anything was out of place or new and I quickly noticed a new addition to the parlour. Kehinde's graduation picture was framed and given pride of place at the top of their LG television. I went to it and picked it up. It had not been there the last time I visited. She was gap-toothed, smiling in her usual innocent way. One hand was on her waist and the other holding the graduation scroll was raised above her head. Most students would look unstylish in the free-sized graduation gown, but Kehinde looked smart in her gown and cap. She always looked good in everything she wore, even if they were drab clothes, but the gown looked like it was made with her size in mind.

"Did you touch up this gown?"

She smiled mischievously, a bit of the old Kehinde I knew showing through the smile. "Just a little. You didn't expect me to wear that garri sack just like that." She winked and held her forefinger to her lips.

"The perks of knowing how to sew." I winked back. "Remember you promised to teach me to sew once we graduated and had time on our hands. Well, we have graduated." I returned the picture to its place and faced her. Her smile disappeared instantly.

She started to speak, stopped and pretended to cough, then tried again. "I don't know if that will be possible now."

Idowu and Bode shuffled out of the room, closing the door behind them. I listened for the sound of their footsteps along the corridor leading to their room and, when I didn't hear anything, I knew they were by the door, eavesdropping.

"Abi, it won't be possible. What was I even thinking? When I resume school next week I won't have the time to learn anymore."

If I was not looking at her face as I spoke I may not have noticed the disbelief that passed through them for a moment before she expertly masked it with animated curiosity.

"Is that the truth?" She was able to infuse the right amount of excitement in her question. I nodded. "That's great. Ehya, congratulations o."

"Thank you o."

An uncomfortable silence followed during which we were both smiling awkwardly. I got some measure of satisfaction at seeing how my news affected her. Surprise and envy, I wanted, not pity and reproach. Feeling accomplished, I stood to leave.

"Oya now. I have to go now."

"Yes, you should before your babies need you."

I wanted to believe her words were innocent and not a low jab to remind me of my mistake, but the smug look on her face made that difficult. I chose to ignore it.

"You haven't even come to see them."

"I will still come. Meanwhile, how will you cope with school and children?"

"We will just have to watch and see."

I took my time leaving after she closed the door behind me. I was convinced they would talk about me once I left and out of curiosity I dragged my feet. As I passed the window of Kehinde's room, on my way to the gate, I heard voices.

"I can't even envy anybody. Who knows what she did to get the admission," Kehinde said in the foreground.

University books were more boring than I imagined. Sitting on our corridor and reading Prof. Okoro's Introduction to Economics, I could hardly keep my eyelids from drooping.

Economics had been my best subject in secondary school and was one of the reasons why I chose it as a course of study in the university. It would be a piece of cake, I thought, but what I was seeing in the book lying open on my lap was completely uninteresting and a lot like the formulae I used to see in the dreaded further maths textbooks. Several times I tried to close the book and take the much needed nap, but each time I remembered I owed it to myself to prove to Prof. Okoro that I was a worthy student, so I kept at it.

I must have lost the struggle against dozing off at some point because Ama's singsong voice startled me out of a deep slumber. I was disoriented at first then focused to see her coming through the gate, her head turned back as she spoke to someone. She held the gate open behind her for the person to come through. When I sighted who it was, my breath caught and I stiffened for a moment, then my heart started racing uncontrollably. Taking deliberate breaths to compose myself, and then feeling adequately calm, I stood and leaned against the railing.

"Are you people just going to stand there?" At the sound of my voice, they turned towards me sharply. Ama smiled and Obinna simply stared and started walking to the veranda. Ama followed.

He walked with grace, always have. It was not the type of gait one acquired from practice and discipline. His was inherent. Right from when he was still a little boy, he walked with an air of self-assurance, like he had all the time in the world to get to his destination, yet with long strides that quickly ate up the distance. As he grew older, age fine-tuned his steps. It could look arrogant to an outsider, especially when it was paired with those eyes that could sometimes look like they were looking at nothing and at other times like they were seeing everything. Those eyes that could settle on you and probe into you until you either wanted to squirm or get lost in them. I was lost then and forgot the good news I wanted to share.

It was unfair that we could not be together again for years. It was especially harder because I had experienced what being with him felt like, what it could be. I tried to change the direction of my thought. My skin heated up, but I knew it had nothing to do with the sun which was already too far in the horizon to have that much effect.

We had promised our parents there would not be a repeat of our shameful behaviour. We were to quit seeing each other privately and

Ama had been implicitly assigned the role of chaperon when I was with him. She cared about us both enough to take her job seriously, so rather than go inside like she usually did upon returning home and allow us the privacy we desperately wanted, she stood with us on the veranda. Her voice brought us out of the depths we were gradually falling into.

"What is that you are holding in your hand?" she asked. Bewildered I looked at her finger, wondering what she just asked me, then followed its direction to the book in my hand.

"Oh, this?" The excitement her curiosity elicited was different from the one that had consumed me just seconds ago, but it was a welcome distraction from the former. I wondered how to break the news and decided to go for the shock factor.

"Professor Okoro, my dean, gave it to me."

They exchanged confused looks then looked at me with furrowed brows.

"What are you talking about?" Obinna came towards me and collected the book. He read the title out loud. "Introduction to Economics. J.N Okoro. How did you get this?"

Ama grabbed the book from his hand too and looked, opening the first page.

"And why is your name written on it?"

"I told you. Professor Okoro gave it to me," I smiled mysteriously, revelling in their confusion.

"Talk joor!" They both screamed in unison.

"I have gotten admission," I screamed too, unable to hold it in any longer.

In response, Ama shook her head and looked genuinely troubled when she said, "Ada, a new list is not out yet. Remember I checked and told you your name wasn't out in the last one?"

"Yes, you did and--" I slapped her arm lightly, "stop looking at me as if I'm mad. My name will be out in the next list."

Ama and Obinna looked at each other again then kept quiet, unsure how to react.

"Okay, it is a good thing to have faith. Hopefully, it will work for you," Obinna said in a patronising tone and, with his arm on my shoulders, gently nudged me into the house. Ama nodded beside him.

I shrugged his arm away. "No, this is not faith. Professor Okoro told me himself and he gave me this book."

"Won't you people leave that girl alone and come inside?" My mother asked from the parlour. "She has gotten admission. Simple! When she's ready to explain to you, she will."

Ama squealed and held onto my left hand, Obinna held the right and they dragged me inside and pushed me into a chair.

"Mummy, good evening ma," they greeted hurriedly and faced me, anticipation animating their features.

"See your faces." Satisfied that their curiosity was adequately aroused, I gave them the lowdown of my visit to their school, making sure to leave no detail out.

Ama's mouth hung open when I was done. As for Obinna, he squeezed my hand and shook his head in wonder. Those eyes, that had the ability to drill into people, looked at me like he was seeing a stranger. The feeling was pleasant.

Chapter Seven

Mother had always looked forward to being a grandmother. "I expect to be a grandma by the time I'm forty," she always sounded it to the hearing of Ama and I. That meant she expected us married and having kids by the time we were 21. She also always loudly envisioned what the thanksgiving ceremony would be like. It would be an extravagant event with all her friends and enemies there; her enemies especially so they could see what her God has done for her.

When Chika and Chuka came along there was no such ceremony, not even a small one to start with, which did not come as a surprise. No one celebrated teenage pregnancy and its outcome. Well-wishers did not troop in like they were wont to upon the arrival of a new child. I had expected it, but it hurt me to know that my children were not celebrated.

They came early, yes, but it was my fault, not theirs and they did not have to suffer for it or be treated like they were not bundles of blessings. I had begun to view them as blessings and wanted everyone else to see them that same way; blessings that came too early, but blessings nonetheless.

True to his word, Professor Okoro pulled some strings on my behalf. The list posted the following Monday confirmed it and Ama quickly shared the good news, calling me on the phone right away while still in front of the notice board. Rather than begin attending lectures immediately, I stayed home that day putting systems in place that would work for me and the kids since I would be away from home a lot. I got the twins registered to an affordable day care centre after I tried and was told they were not qualified for the free day care available to staff of mother's school, where Chukwuemeka went. When that was sorted out, I completed plans with Ama for our birthday which was in three days' time.

We were not meant to have a big celebration, but I was thinking of other things.

Thursday dawned with a bit of a bite in the air. Harmattan announced itself that morning. I remembered how rainy it had been the previous year, with no sign of harmattan. It was not just my birthday, it was also the day the seeds that would change my life forever were sown.

Ama and Obinna returned from school very early, just a little past midday, and joined in preparations. It was supposed to be just a gathering of less than twenty people but they had both invited their friends. I had very few people I could call friends to invite.

At six thirty p.m., after my parents left for evening Mass from where they would proceed to join the Charismatic prayer meeting, the first of our guests began to arrive. To my surprise, some of our friends from secondary school showed up at Ama's invitation. They smiled at me uncomfortably, made great efforts to avoid eye contact and enquired about the twins who were in their room sleeping.

A number of Ama's new friends from university were also there, but it was Obinna's friends who made up a larger part of the crowd. He had always been an outgoing person who handled the social scene quite well, so it was no surprise.

There was no particular order to the party, just a group of people enjoying the latest songs, chatting, eating and having fun. Our parlour which always appeared enormous to me, seemed small then with all the bodies milling around it. Those from my secondary school sat together talking in hushed tones and sipping the soft drinks Ama served. She stayed a while with them then moved on to her new friends from the university, chatting animatedly with each group. Though I could not hear her, her head and hands moved around a lot. At intervals, she would hit her hand against her lap repeatedly while her head lolled backwards as she laughed without guise. I realised it was the same way she used to be with the other crowd from secondary school, but had moved on fast to a new one. Though she had not noticed, I could feel the change. She had become closer with these people she had known for only a few weeks, while the bond with those we spent six years of secondary school with was thinning.

Determined to ensure everyone was comfortable, I took one of the bowls of fried meat set up on the dining table and went to the corner where the past students of Great Heights International College were huddled, a very friendly smile plastered on my face. As I got close enough for my presence to be noticed, their conversation ebbed until they were silently staring at their feet, hands, the muted television, each other, everywhere but at me. These were the ones with whom I used to spend hours talking about everything and laughing the way Ama was now laughing with her new friends until my stomach muscles became taut. That was then. They were now strangers.

I put the bowl of meat on a side stool, stood around for a few seconds until I could not bear the uneasiness anymore. No wonder Ama could no longer stand them, I thought as I turned to leave and consoled myself in the knowledge that the party would be over in about one hour thirty minutes maximum. The clock above their heads showed we were only forty-five minutes into the party.

A hand on my arm stopped me before I could put enough space between me and them. "Can we see your babies?"

I looked at the hand on my arm then looked up into the face of Kingsley with the intention of telling him off, but the smile and genuineness in his eyes softened the hard glint in mine, although I had every reason to doubt that he meant well.

When we just became seniors in S.S.1 and students began pairing off, he had been the first boy to voice his interest in me. It was break time and I was in my chair reading the English language novel for that term, *Violence,* when he came up and sat on the desk beside me, one long leg on the floor and the other on the chair. I wanted to scold him for putting his muddy shoe on the chair, but the anxious look in his eyes and his body language educed my sympathy. For a long time, I sensed he was interested in me and was still working up the courage to tell me how he felt. Call it the female intuition, but the way he always seemed uncomfortable around me and frequently aimed to please was sign enough.

I looked up then, my eyes enquiring. He opened his mouth to speak, stuttered then rubbed his palm across his nose and stopped. I felt sympathetic and decided to make it easy for him.

"Are you not going for break?" This was a safe conversation starter, so I took it.

"I already sent someone to get things for me. Are you not going?" he threw my question back at me.

Ama and I had bought a saving box built out of wood and were saving to buy a sewing machine similar to Kehinde's. To achieve that, we agreed to spend only one person's pocket money each day. It was Ama's money to be spent on that day, which meant she went on break and shared whatever she bought between us. In the same way, when going home one of us would carry the other in the bus and save on transport fare as well. The sacrifice we made was telling on the weight of our saving box, but I could not tell all that to Kingsley Iheanacho.

"Ama is buying for me," I answered.

"It must feel extraordinary being a twin."

It was a statement I had heard so many times in my life and I was tired of explaining that it did not feel unusual or wonderful, but perfectly normal, maybe as normal as it felt for those who were not twins. It was the only way I had known since I was born, so it did not feel different.

Rather than go into that long explanation which was always followed

58

by an equally long argument, I chose to agree with him. "Yes, it feels extraordinary."

Conversation exhausted, we settled into silence. I raised the novel, pretending I could read beyond one line, while he shuffled his foot continuously on the chair.

"I wanted to ask you something." The words came out slowly, like they were being forced out of him.

"What?" I did not bother to look up from my book. The fact that my eyes were not trained on him seemed to give him courage.

"Will you be my girl?" I looked up then and he shrugged like he was apologising and pleading for a favourable answer at the same time.

"No," I said with a smile. He looked like he did not believe my answer. My smile must have given the impression that I was being unserious.

"What?"

"I said no. I don't want to date anybody until S.S.3." I do not remember deciding on that, but as I said it I knew that was what it would be.

"But that's still too far," he protested.

"Yes. And that's the way I want it. I don't want distractions, Kingsley. I'm sorry."

Ama's entrance stopped whatever he was going to say next and he left. But he did not relent. Every opportunity he had he used it to woo me, sometimes sending his friends to talk to me, buying me gifts on Valentine's Day and visiting me in the school's sick bay with frozen yogurt the day I was sick in school. Still, my reply to him was always negative.

Not that he was not the type of boy a girl would like to be with, but I really did not want to have a relationship in school, though most people had at least one before graduating. I was already aware enough to know that most relationships formed in school led nowhere and ended upon graduation. I also knew that my parents would not approve.

For the next two and a half years we continued in this fashion, with him trying to win me over and me evading, so when I became pregnant I imagined him mocking me and gloating behind my back. It was what I expected anyone in his shoes to do, such that my expectation took form and I began to see that as reality even though I had no evidence.

But as I searched his face that night, I realised I had not heard any rumour about him making such a statement, and I did hear a good number of the rumours making the rounds from my sisters who were in the same school. I saw no reason to refuse his request to see the babies.

I gestured for him to come with me and began moving toward the rooms. At the door that would take us out of the parlour and into the inner part of the house, I turned and saw not only Kingsley but every one of my former classmates following me. I frowned and stopped, turning fully to face them, my arms folded across my chest.

"We want to see too naa," Feyi, who was never my friend but was friends with Ama, pouted and mirrored my pose. The others nodded their agreement. I did not have to think for long, after all I had been planning to turn the last thirty minutes of the party into a thanksgiving ceremony of sorts for the twins, to make up for the lack of one hitherto. I let them in.

They all crowded into the room, chattering excitedly, to be met by a stern looking Nnenna who stopped them with a scowl and a finger to her lips.

"Shhh. Don't you know you should not shout where babies are sleeping?"

I wanted to laugh at the scenario. The junior scolding the seniors. Though now a senior herself in S.S.1, the former Nnenna would never have been able to talk that way to them, as though they were peers. They were three classes ahead of her and could very easily have found a reason to punish her back at school, but I had a feeling that even if we were all still students of Great Heights International, that would not have deterred the girl Nnenna had grown into from speaking her mind. It was not just me who had become mature with the arrival of the twins. Nnenna had come to take her role as aunty seriously and was constantly acting the part.

She left the room then, unfazed by their collective disapproving gaze, and gently closed the door my guests left open.

As soon as she was gone, they crowded around the cots, making comments about the features of the babies and how cute they looked. Looking closer, I noticed beads of sweat dotting Chika's face then my eyes went to the windows. Nnenna, in her zeal to keep the babies warm, left the windows closed and the fans off. I hit the switch and cool breeze circulated.

"Your son is so fair, like you and your mum. The girl looks like she's going to have your dad's dark skin. Or maybe she took it from her dad. Is her dad dark?" His little finger wrapped in Chuka's hand, Kingsley looked at me, his eyes enquiring.

I did not feel I owed him an answer so I evaded the question. "Well, Chika was fair when she was born but she's been getting darker. They keep changing every day."

"And she has your full hair," Feyi pointed out. "See, her hair is almost reaching her eyebrows."

After a while, I led them out of the room. In the parlour I saw Ama had brought out the cake and her friends were blended with Obinna's friends, all of them chatting like they did not just meet. Immediately Obinna saw me he motioned for me to join him.

"You people should meet Ada, my *very* good friend." Most of his friends cleared their throat at the emphasis on *very*, teasing him. Ignoring them he drew me closer with his arm on my shoulders and introduced his friends to me, one after the other. I tried to keep up with all the names he rattled off, but the effort left me slightly disoriented.

They were a boisterous group. I was immediately drawn into their crowd and soon I was enjoying the party better than I did earlier, such that time flew by without my noticing it.

Twenty minutes to the end of the party, I lowered the volume of the music to get my guests' attention. Everyone in the room turned to me, expectant. I inhaled deeply and decided I would give the twins the ceremony they deserved. It may not be as elaborate as it should have been under normal circumstances, but I would have stories to tell them when they grew up about what their thanksgiving ceremony was like. They would know they were wanted and appreciated when they were born.

"I have an announcement to make," I began.

Obinna, like everyone else, was smiling at me with those soulful eyes. I wondered if he remembered what other anniversary the day marked. He had not mentioned it. We rarely ever discussed anything intimate because we were deliberately making efforts to avoid getting closer than was advisable. When we had time to ourselves after the party I would remind him.

Still looking at Obinna, and drawing strength from his presence, I continued, "Some of you are aware that I was blessed with two wonderful gifts." His smile faltered and he shook his head slightly. This caused me to stop. His eyes shifted, warning me. I realized that meant he did not want me talking about it, but I could not understand why.

"Go on, you've counted your blessings, now name them one by one," Kanu, one of the friends Obinna introduced me to earlier, encouraged me, a hearty laughter following his words.

I laughed. "As I said, the blessings are two in number and of course I'll name them; Chika and Chuka are the babies…" In the crowd I saw Ama's mouth open. She waved her hand for me to cut it out, unfortunately I felt it was already too late. "…God has given me twins and I want this party to also be a small thanksgiving ceremony for them," I concluded.

I was not sure what I was expecting them to do next, but the silence that descended in the sitting room was certainly not it. Apart from those I went to school with, most of the guests socializing in my parlour and eating my birthday cake did not know I was a mother.

"Hey, I have an announcement to make too. I'm pregnant with triplets." Kanu snorted and pointed to his beer belly. "I think I will name them Athos, Porthos and Aramis. Musketeer babies."

The laughter that followed was lengthier than the first. He obviously thought I was joking and only realized his error when he noticed no one was laughing along. That stopped him abruptly. The tension in the room was of such intensity that I felt vibrations in my ear, but worse than that was the sense of loss and the feeling of loneliness. For the first time, I felt like I had no one on my side. Ama's disapproving shake of head said more than words that this once I was on my own. Almost every eye in the room stole glances at Obinna. Though I had not mentioned who fathered the children, I saw they already knew from his countenance. His eyes were still fixed on me, betrayal visible in them. That elicited a similar feeling within me. The chill started from my feet then spread all through my body, causing my skin to break out in goose bumps at the realization that he was ashamed of his children.

"Congratulations. Thank God for safe delivery." Kingsley's voice breaking the silence sounded strained, so was his wide smile. Others joined in offering their congratulations.

"Congratulations. Can we see them?" The girl Obinna had intro-duced as Deola asked with a hand on my arm. The tenderness in her touch almost made me smile and offer to show her into the children's room when I noticed Obinna stomp out. Ama went after him.

"Maybe another time, Deola," I said.

To fight the tears clouding my vision and threatening to fall, I took quick breaths, unable to say anything to the confused faces looking at me for a clue on what to do next. It was easy to see they all wanted to leave and put an end to the awkward situation but only stayed out of courtesy.

Ama returned then, alone.

"Thank you all so much for coming to celebrate with us today," she said, her gaze taking in everyone in the room. In her polite way, she dis-missed them, bringing the party to an end. Feet that needed no further encouragement shuffled out in a hurry.

When I thought the parlour had emptied, I sat on a chair and rested my forehead on the heels of my palms.

"Everything will be fine." Kingsley's soothing voice pulled me out of the abyss of self-pity I was sinking into. I looked into his eyes. I could see empathy there, and something that I needed more than anything else, understanding. I began to wonder what my reasons were for refusing him all through school. Thanking him and explaining that I needed to be alone; I stood and walked him to the door. I absently heard him mention something about getting admission and leaving for school soon, but nothing really registered.

Obinna was standing outside, leaning against the railing on the corridor. I thought he had gone too, but when he turned and looked at me I knew he would not leave without a confrontation. I braced myself for it and went back inside. He followed.

"You could at least have warned us of what you were planning," Ama scolded.

"My own children kwa? Ama, I don't need permission," I returned with the same heat.

"Your children only? You could at least have warned me," Obinna stabbed his chest with his forefinger.

"You make it sound like introducing your children to the world is a disaster you had to be prepared for."

"There would have been a time for that, just not now," he lashed out angrily, his voice loud. Ama gestured for him to lower his voice then pointed in the direction of the children's room.

"There would have been a time for me to get pregnant too, just not now," I flung back at him. "It wasn't convenient, yet I stepped into the role when the time came."

"Well if you were sensible enough you wouldn't have gotten pregnant."

Immediately the words were out, he covered his mouth with his palm and looked contrite.

"How dare you!" Ama stepped in front of him and pushed him with both hands on his chest.

"I'm sorry. It's just that I have a reputation to protect," he replied.

It would not have shocked me as much if he had smashed my face into the wall. The chill I felt earlier crept deeper inside my skin, surrounding my heart and squeezing like a fist.

I spoke as calmly as I could manage. "Obinna, why don't you go ahead and protect your rep? I will make it easier for you; you will no longer see these children or have anything to do with them." I went to the door and opened it. "You can leave now and make sure you stay away."

Obinna gave a short bark of laughter, but there was no mirth in it. It was more of a warning. As if to challenge me, he moved, but not toward the door I held open. He went further inside and I followed, prepared to enlist the help of my sisters to throw him out. I entered to meet him bent over Chika's bed kissing her. He did the same with Chuka and even Chukwuemeka, then without a glance at me, he left the room.

I returned to the parlour after I was sure he had gone to find Ama packing away the dishes.

"Ada…" she started, but I stopped her with a raised palm and my face turned away. Though she stood up to Obinna eventually, I was upset that she agreed with him about keeping the children secret.

My younger sisters came out together, looking at us for clarification. Nnenna made for the half-eaten cake, cut a slice and hissed loudly. "Obinna should thank his stars that I'm not you," she said before tossing the generous slice into her mouth.

Overwrought nerves had me arranging all the clothes I would need for one week on one side of my closet where it would be easy to reach each morning. I did same with my bag; putting everything I felt would be needed the next day into the only handbag I owned. I was exhausted by the time I was done, yet, I still was not calm enough to settle down and fall asleep.

The children's room did not provide the peace it usually gave when I went in there with the aim of putting together everything they needed for their first day at day care, which was the following day. Hardly had I brought out the large brown bag reserved for that when I broke down and dumped the bag hard on the floor. The clothes, diapers and bibs fell out and scattered across the room. Obinna's words re-echoed, *if you were sensible enough you wouldn't have gotten pregnant.*

Anger made my body quake so much that I had to hold on to the open drawer from where I had been taking out clothes and fought for control. He does not deserve me, I concluded to make myself feel less awful. He certainly does not deserve to be a father, not if he is unwilling to accept responsibilities for his actions and live with the consequences, which included accepting that he has kids already and they could not be hidden from the world. If he wanted to keep them a secret I would help him do that as best as I could.

My chest heaved faster the more I agonised over his words. Emotions rose, starting from the region where my heart is located, to pool in my eyes and almost spilled out in form of tears. Sliding down to the floor, I tried hard to hold on to the anger and not give in to self-loathing. Anger, I could handle. It helped to think of him as the one in the wrong. I convinced myself that it was all mostly his fault, not mine.

He had made the first move that day last year. Last year now seemed like so many years ago. It was hard to believe that it was only one year since he had looked at me like I was the only being that mattered in the whole world and said the sweetest words to me, words that made me throw away all the principles I ever stood for and give in to a pleasure which had now morphed into pain and heartaches. The Obinna I had seen just moments ago was a totally different person; a person I never wanted to see. I would make sure of that. It did not matter that we were going to the same school. As far as I was concerned Obinna and I had no business together, his words had sliced through my core and I would not give him a chance to hurt me that way ever again. It was a pity that we were bound together forever by the children we shared. That was my only regret. A sigh emanating from one of the cots had me revising my opinion. No, I had no regrets, not about the children. Every moment with them had been a treasure and I would not regret it. The only regret was the person I chose to father them, coupled with the wrong timing.

Too tired to rise from my position on the floor, I crawled to the twin cot and looked at Chika and Chuka, drawing strength from them. Their features were no longer as delicate as they had been. They had filled out and were now less identical than they were at birth. Chuka was chubbier.

True to his sex, his mouth worked every waking hour, always looking for something to suckle on. As long as he was feeding he was content. His mouth moved then, like he was suckling. That brought the first genuine smile of the evening to my face. Feeling calmer, I passed my fingers through the thick black mass covering his head and curling round his ears, nape, and forehead. It was extremely soft. I did not want to take my hand away even though some of the oil from the Pears baby oil applied after his evening bath stayed on my fingers. That was something he and his sister still had in common; thick, soft mane and the same round shaped face. Chika, though chubby, was much slimmer than her brother. The single light bulb on the ceiling cast shadows of her lashes over her cheeks. Apart from those long lashes, her eyes looked ordinary as she slept. When she was awake those dark brown eyes darted about looking at everything inquisitively, while her expressive face exuded all the wonder and curiosity she could not yet express with words.

I became aware that while I watched them, peace had overtaken the fury I had brought with me into the room. Obinna could be gone for all I cared, all that mattered lay in this cot.

The door opened as I rose to finish packing their bag. It was my mother, still in the native caftan and matching scarf she wore out. She obviously just got home and I assumed she had come to check on the children.

"They are sleeping," I told her hoping she would leave me to my solitude and retire into her room. I did not want company just yet, especially my mother's. She could sense even the best hidden emotions and I was not ready to answer any questions.

"Prepare, we are going to Mama Obinna's house."

Instantly my head snapped up same time as my hand stopped folding.

"For what?" I asked.

I sensed that Obinna had told his parents what happened and they called my parents. I did not expect him to act in such manner. It baffled me that he did not have the sense to realize he could not keep running to mummy for every little thing now that he was a parent himself.

"We need to talk to both of you." She remained at the door, not bothering to come in.

"This night?" Both our eyes moved to the clock. 09:59 p.m.

"Are you going to stay there, asking me questions? You better hurry, your father is still outside waiting in the car," she said and left the room.

In less than 3 minutes, we were in the Onwukas' compound on Jadesola Oshodi Street, just behind Efutide Street.

I was reluctant to enter Obinna's home with my parents. They had gone in immediately my father parked his Mercedes-Benz v-boot behind Obinna's father's own, which was the same model. Both our fathers had gone to buy the cars, together, on the same day, a day I remembered.

With the excuse of calling Ama to check on the children, I stayed outside a while longer. The compound was always neat. With the exception of a few leaves which often fell from the orange tree close to the fence, it was rare to see any dirt on the floor of their yard. I often chalked it up to the absence of kids in the compound. Even their cars were parked in an orderly manner, by the side of the building, close to the right fence that separated their house from their neighbour's. The opposite fence, where the orange tree was, had white plastic chairs arranged around a white plastic table, with a large white umbrella rising from a hole in the middle of the table. As with every part of the house, not one chair was out of place. If I had not met the family entertaining visitors there on some days I would never have believed anyone used them.

From this spot, one could see a dog cage further down, by the side of the building. Jack and Jimmy sat in there, tongues hanging out, waiting to be let out. The cage was also tidy. It was rare that one saw dog droppings or leftover food in there. The dogs were well trained and could respond to orders, unlike most other dogs I had come across in the neighbourhood. They were fierce though, Jack especially, and for that reason, they were mostly caged, except when the family was about to retire for the night, then they were left to roam free. I often wondered why they needed the barbed wires surrounding their fence. The dogs were enough protection. They barked then, excitedly, and I longed to go to them like I used to. It had been a long time since I played with them. Come to think of it, it had been a long time since I played at all.

"They are waiting for you." Obinna's gruff voice sliced through what little calm I had attained from watching the dogs. Standing in the corridor, surrounded by the harsh light of the white fluorescent bulb directly above him, his face looked even angrier than when he left my house. Good, I thought, he should stay angry. He does not deserve any happiness. I knew he could not see my face clearly through the darkness outside, the moon was not full enough for a bright night, yet I wore a scowl to match his. If he wanted to frown I would show him I was better at it. I waited for him to go in, then I followed.

Once inside, I regretted my decision to wait a while longer. Both our parents had occupied all the other chairs and the only space left for me was with Obinna on the three seater couch. He was spread out in the middle so that no matter how I sat I would be close to him.

His parents responded to my greeting while I went to perch on the arm of the chair occupied by my mother. She frowned at me. I noticed she wasn't the only one giving me a disapproving look, yet I stayed put. A stern look from adults was better than sitting beside that child.

"Ada, there is space there for you to sit." My mother indicated the spaces on either sides of Obinna then jerked her head to the side, a gesture for me to move there. I stood and went to the couch.

"Shift." I spoke in the same gruff tone he had used when he asked me to come inside.

"Move, or adjust," my mother corrected.

"Shift," I said again beneath my breath so my mother will not hear. Ignoring my request he pointed with both hands to the spaces beside him.

"Will you sit down let's start what we came here for?" My father scolded.

I sat immediately on the side stool by the far side of the couch and bent my head, braced for another scolding. Thankfully none came.

"Happy birthday Ada and congratulations on your admission," Uncle Silas said without preamble, his voice hearty as always.

"Thank you, uncle." I looked up briefly, then back at my feet.

"Hope you enjoyed your party?" Obinna's mother asked. I nodded without looking up. I had a feeling she already knew how the party went. Her son had, no doubt, given her the details, so why ask again?

I wanted to return home, to the comfort and familiarity of my bed. This house, though familiar, no longer felt welcoming. The pictures of Obinna and his family, hanging at different spots on the wall, were not suitably entertaining or distracting, not even the one of a tearful Obinna standing behind a table with a cake in the shape of the number 1 and a single candle on top.

I always teased Obinna about that picture and some other unflattering ones of him at different stages of his life. Now the pictures didn't look so endearing anymore. Where I always thought I saw innocence, I now saw cruelty beneath the shy smiles. The mouth opened to say, "Cheese" now seemed to be saying, "Why were you stupid enough to get pregnant?" Why did I ever think he was cute?

"Good." Uncle Silas leaned forward in his chair. I noticed my mother imitate his movement. He opened his mouth but was stopped by the loud clang of aluminium kitchenware hitting the ground. We all looked toward the kitchen.

"Nkechi!" Aunty Oyedinma called.

A young girl came to the door linking the kitchen to the parlour. From her physique, I figured she was in her early teens, though I couldn't be certain about it. Her head was bent forward, hiding her face. She worried her fingers so much I expected them to fall off any minute. Hers was a new face, but it was no surprise. The Onwukas changed domestic helps almost as often as they replenished their foodstuff. All it took was for Aunty Oyedinma to see grease on an already washed plate or step foot on sand in the house. She never raised her voice or nagged, she simply acted by replacing the offending help.

"What are you still doing in the kitchen?" Mrs Onwuka asked. Nkechi's reply was to start biting her lips in addition to wringing her fingers. "You can go and sleep now."

Though dismissed, Nkechi did not seem too eager to leave her post in the kitchen and turned to return there.

"Is there something you kept in that kitchen?" Mrs Onwuka stopped her before she could disappear inside.

Nkechi shook her head.

"Then go to bed, not when morning comes you'll be waiting for me to come and beg you to wake up."

Mr Onwuka promptly continued his speech as soon as Nkechi left.

"Ada we are happy for you that you have gotten admission into school, but we are also very worried."

My heart suddenly beating faster, I risked looking at his face. He looked thoughtful and that worried me. So many thoughts rushed through at once; were they going to ask me to give up the admission for the sake of the kids? It was a possibility considering that I had yet to pay the acceptance fee.

"Worried how?" My voice shook. I looked at my mother for explanation, but her face was blank.

Obinna's mother stood abruptly then gestured for her husband to continue talking while she walked stealthily to the door which led into the rooms, the same door Nkechi had passed a moment ago.

"Both of you going to the same school ..."

Mrs Onwuka opened the door suddenly and Nkechi stumbled face first into the parlour. I turned to find her eyes looking around confused, like a rat caught in a trap and looking for a means of escape.

"I want to see you going into your room now," Mrs Onwuka pointed in the direction of her room. The girl scuttled off, oblivious that that was most likely her last night in the house. We all knew Mrs Onwuka enough to know that the girl would not get another chance to misbehave.

"We do not want a repeat of what happened before." My father took over from where Uncle Silas stopped as soon as Mrs Onwuka returned to her seat.

"Yes," Obinna's father picked up the conversation. "We have done what we can to keep you away from each other, but being in the same school means we will have no control over what you do."

"I have learnt my lesson. There's no way I will make the same mistake twice," I said earnestly.

Obinna seemed unconcerned by what was about to happen. He was not the one about to lose his chance at being a university undergraduate.

"We really hope you have." Obinna's mother said. "But you cannot blame us if the trust we have for you is no longer as strong."

"True. I promise nothing like this will ever happen again. Please." I lost control and a tear dropped.

"Ọgini? Why are you now crying?" My mother asked confused.

"Don't stop me from going to school."

"No, no, no. Nobody is going to do that." Obinna's father said gently. I looked at him, doubtful. "We just need to be sure that we are not making a mistake by letting the two of you have so much freedom."

"You are going to have to promise us, both of you," my father pointed to Obinna and me, "that you will not go to school and start from where you stopped."

Relief coursed through me, leaving me speechless. No one was going to ask me to give up school for the time being.

At our silence my father moved to the edge of his seat and steepled his fingers. "I see you are not ready to make the promise."

"I promise," I said and looked at Obinna, willing him to speak.

"You promise to do what?" My mother prompted.

"I promise not to bring disgrace to our families again."

There was silence as all eyes turned to Obinna, waiting for him to speak. When he finally did it was with his eyes on me.

"If you are worried that what happened before will repeat itself you don't have to be. There can *never* be anything between us again," he said with more heat than I thought was necessary.

His words stung. For a while, it seemed I was the only one who noticed it until I saw my mother. Rather than look reassured she was scowling at Obinna.

"Nna, you know you don't have a choice. There will always be something between the two of you. Whether you like it or not you've both created something that will last for a lifetime. I hope you know that?"

My heart bloated at the unexpected solidarity, causing my breath to quicken. Gratitude for her loyalty merged with a feeling of unworthiness. I didn't deserve it, yet she stood by me.

"Yes, aunty." Obinna lowered his head and managed to look contrite. Our parents looked at us but said nothing.

When Obinna's mother started to speak, I held my breath fearing an altercation but none came.

"I still think we should let my driver use my old Volvo to take her and the twins to and from school on week days. It will make things easier, if not for her, at least for the children." She addressed my parents, her husband nodding his support, but my parents were already refusing before she was done.

"No, Mama Obinna. Let it be as we agreed. Between her and me, we will work out a schedule for dropping the children at day care. She doesn't need a driver. Even I, her mother, I do not have a car of my own. Let her struggle like other students before she starts thinking she did a good thing by getting pregnant."

My father was nodding enthusiastically. "She said the truth. Are you going to pamper her now? If it is going to be stressful, let her suffer it. That is life."

He stopped addressing Mrs Onwuka and turned to me. "You live with the result of your decisions. Have you heard?"

I nodded slightly.

"Now I think we better start going. It's already late," said my father.

Chapter Eight

Following directions, I walked into what I believed to be the Economics class for first year students and wondered if there was a mistake. I was nervous about being the new girl, walking into a class that had started receiving lectures four weeks earlier. I had never been the new girl, having gone to just one primary and secondary school where I resumed together with the first set of students, so I did not know how to act as a new student.

All through secondary school, I had watched new students join us, and noticed how hard it was for them to blend in. Relationships had already been formed, cliques tightly knit, so that breaking in took great courage. Some eventually adjusted and blended in with other students, but some never did and continued to be outsiders. I worried I might be among the latter.

However, the scene that greeted me made me wonder if I had just wandered into a kindergarten class with babies the size of grown men and women. There were more students seated on the tables than there were on chairs, and even more standing around, each group talking in loud tones so as to be heard above the din. For a moment, I compared the situation I just walked into to the one I left a few minutes ago when I dropped the children off at day care, and found the day care had been quieter and organised. The discomfort I felt earlier vanished, replaced by disappointment: is this what the much-touted higher institution and the freedom we longed to enjoy once we got there, was all about?

I dodged gesticulating bodies as I looked around, trying to decide which seat to take. At the far end of the room, on the first row, I noticed a girl sitting alone, her head bent over a book, oblivious to the confusion going on around her, and picked my way towards her. I figured she had to be new. Perhaps, like me, her name just came out and it was her first week in class. She didn't look up when I sat; didn't even act like she noticed when my bag brushed her arm. The apology I gave was not acknowledged either. I gave up trying to be civilised and dug out books and a pen from my bag to begin writing.

I had barely gone past two lines when I felt the need to look up. I did into a smiling, curiously familiar face standing a few feet away. Holding the smile, she started walking in my direction, while I wracked my brain frantically to figure out where I knew her from before she got to me. I could not. I had been afraid that all eyes would be on me when I came into the class, now I was grateful for even just one face giving me attention.

"Hello, Ada." She lowered herself to the table and lifted both legs to the chair. I shifted, slightly, so my dress wouldn't get caught beneath her shoe soles. Unsure how to address her, I smiled back and waited for her to explain.

"I know you don't remember me." Luckily there was no anger or accusation in her voice, just a hint of amusement. "Who will blame you? It's easier for a crowd to remember one person than for one person to recognise the entire crowd, and it was a crowd you had in your house last night."

The mention of last night brought back memories of how the night had ended and my face burned with shame at that recollection.

"Oh," was all I could manage. When the silence stretched toward awkwardness, I had to ask, "You must be Ama's course mate then. What are you doing here?" I deduced she had to be Ama's friend for her to have been invited.

"This is my class." She leaned forward and picked up the book I was writing from. "And this is my book."

From the first day Ama brought books home, borrowed from a first year Economics student to help me keep up ahead of admission with what was being taught, I often tried to imagine what the owner of the book looked like whenever I flipped through the pages. This Kosisochukwu Chima, would she look as disorganised as her handwriting? It was always an effort to understand what she wrote. She scribbled like writing was a race, something one had to hurry through, without necessarily understanding it. I mostly had to squint or employ intuition to decipher what she put down. Unfortunately, hers was the only note Ama brought home for all the subjects. It was better than none at all.

Finally meeting her, she was the antithesis of her writing. While her notes were dog-eared with illegible handwriting and lots of badly done cancellations, she was very well put together. From the neat rows of Ghana braids to the well-filed nails that glistened with nail hardener, she looked perfect. There was no wrinkle on her red cotton shirt, the matching red ballet flats on the chair looked like she had been carried into the class and didn't walk through the dusty path which led to our class.

"Your sister invited me and some other of our friends," she explained.

Understanding dawned then and with it a new source of anxiety.

"Kosi, was there anyone else from this class at my house last night?"

She shrugged narrow shoulders and threw a carefree hand in the air as she said, "No. Just me."

My sigh of relief was instantaneous and that drew laughter from her.

"I don't think you should feel bad about yesterday. I think you did the right thing." She stood then and dusted the bottom of her jean trousers. "I admire your courage. Shift," she nudged me with her hip.

"Adjust," I corrected her before I could think, then quickly apologised when she raised her brows in mild amusement.

"What are you? English teacher?" She said this without malice and reached behind her to dig out a folded exercise book from the pocket of her jean before sitting down. She was a contrast, I observed, paying special attention to her appearance but next to none to her books. I stopped myself before I could go into a lecture about how she needed to care for her books.

"Don't mind me, jare. I forgot myself," I answered.

Soon enough, there was an increase in activity, with students jumping down from tables to hurriedly settle into chairs. A measure of calm took over and it became my idea of what a university class should be. In front of the class stood a lanky man who moved straight to the board and, saying nothing, started to scrawl on it. I had expected him to reprimand the students for being so rowdy, but his indifference told me it was normal behaviour for university students to be unruly.

Another surprise came when he started teaching. I watched him write ACC 101 then, still facing the board, he plunged into a long narrative, mostly reading from the book in his hand, occasionally writing on the board, never once turning to gauge the reaction of the students behind him. In a rush, he read through one page then turned to the other. Occasionally, the sound of rustling papers filled the room as the students kept up with him in the exercise of page turning. I felt a nudge at my side then Kosi pushed a textbook in front of my face, pointing to the line where he was.

"Excuse me, sir," I called out before I realised I planned to, breaking into the monotony of his voice. Kosi pulled at my hand that was raised in the air. I heard giggles then Kosi's voice shushing me, but it was already late. He was turning. Disbelief flashed in his eyes as they settled on me.

"Yes?" There was so much said with that single word.

"Sir, I don't understand anything," I replied. A warning murmur rose in the class. Kosi pinched me under the table.

"So what are you doing here?" He left his place by the board and started toward me. "How did you pass JAMB? This is how we know those who got in here through special centres and those who paid to have their name on the admission list."

I shook my head denying all his accusations but he was not finished.

"Which mushroom secondary school did you go to? Was it even government approved?" With each humiliating question he threw at me the snicker among the students increased, fuelling my frustration. This frustration emboldened me. He was now directly in front of me. It angered me even further to feel my throat tighten and know that tears of humiliation were close.

"Sir, that is why I'm here… to learn. If I knew everything I wouldn't be here," I croaked over the tightness and bent my head, braced for what would come after.

There was a long moment of silence during which I thought I would pass out from holding my breath. He spoke eventually. "This is a student who knows what she came here for."

I wasn't sure I heard correctly. I raised my head to see him addressing the class and pointing at me. I was certain there was a catch. I held my breath again, waiting for the rebuke to come, but he turned to me and asked softly, "So what don't you understand?"

The next four hours were spent sitting through lectures from lecturers more interested in covering more topics than in imparting knowledge. Not wanting to create a scene like I did earlier, I sat still, flipping through pages I did not understand and, taking a cue from the other students, answered in the affirmative when any lecturer stopped to ask if we understood. The lecturer often continued lecturing before we finished answering.

When our secondary school teachers, while telling us what to expect when in university, said that we would be on our own, I thought they meant being free to do as we pleased. After one day in university, I was beginning to understand it to mean that we were left on our own when it came to teaching ourselves. So why bother to come for lectures anyway when we could just buy the hand-outs and read?

I said as much to Kosi as she walked with me to Mr Okoro's office after lectures.

"Maybe I should just stay at home and come to school only when we have a test or something. I could call you and you'll tell me how many chapters they covered every day and I'll read on my own."

"Ha! Do you think you are the only one that has that kind of sense? If it were possible no one will be coming for lectures, unless for test and exams. That's why they started taking attendance. If you don't attend up to seventy percent of the lectures for each course, you won't be qualified to sit for that exam."

"Oh," I said as understanding dawned. "No wonder."

"Ehn hen. I heard people were skipping lectures anyhow. In one class you might see only twenty students then when exam starts you'll be surprised to find more than three times the students you normally see in class, so they had to make attendance compulsory."

Still unwilling to believe there was no way around it, I started thinking of other ways to beat the system so I could stay away from the lectures I considered pointless.

"What if someone signs the attendance list for me?"

"Well people do that too, but the lecturers, their eyes have opened too. That is why they don't say when there will be a test. They could come to class any day and just ask you to tear a sheet of paper."

"Ehn, then you call me and I'll hurry down."

"Hurry down from where? All the way from Surulere to Yaba? If you were living in the hostel you might even consider that, though it doesn't really work for those in the hostel anymore. Once they announce a test they stop letting students into their class, until after the test. My dear, there's no way around it. We are stuck with their boring lectures. All we now pray for is that they miss their lectures. In fact, we look forward to it."

We reached the front of the Dean's office. "But wait oh, you just resumed today and you are already tired of lectures. Are you that unserious?"

"Considering how long I waited to get into university, I never knew I'd be tired of it so soon, but it's just not what I thought it would be," I explained. "The lectures are not serious enough for me to leave my children with strangers."

Kosi's hand reached for the door handle. I stopped her before she could open it and pulled her aside.

"Kosi…" I hesitated then felt foolish for it. "Please don't tell anyone about my children. I don't want people to know about them…yet."

"OK." She shrugged. "I won't." I was relieved she did not ask questions or try to communicate her opinion on the matter.

Professor Okoro's secretary did not bother to look up when I came in. With her gaze fixed on the paper she was typing from, she appeared irritated at being interrupted. Her tone when she told me, "Professor Okoro is not around" confirmed it.

"Ok, I'll wait for - "

"No." her head whipped up before I could finish my sentence. When her eyes narrowed, I knew she recognised me and I started to smile.

"You again?" she said in an accusatory tone that caused my smile to disappear. She stood from her desk and came around to meet me before I could blink. "You can't stay." She held my arm and tried to lead me out, but I dug my heels in. "Oya, come and start going," she said pointing at the door.

"I need to see Professor Okoro."

"And I said you cannot see him. What is your problem?" She asked slapping both palms together for emphasis. "That is how you came the other time and I almost lost my job, now you want me to get into trouble again ehn? If you want to see Professor Okoro, book an appointment." She clapped her hands together again in that habit of hers, this time though she wouldn't stop. "Come and be going." As she spoke her eye kept darting toward the door in panic.

"Ok. I want to book an appointment."

"You cannot." When I frowned at her, she frowned back and moved closer to me, feet planted apart and hands on her waist, her stance depicting one who was ready for trouble. "It seems you are a trouble maker. Only lecturers can book appointment to see Professor Okoro. Students can see him in class if they want to. You come to his office only if he asks you to."

She moved away from me and went to the door, opening it. "Leave now."

I glimpsed Kosi's confused face in the corridor, through the opened door, just before I said, "I came to pay him his money," then the door closed immediately, shutting her out.

Abike leaned against the door, eyeing me with suspicion. "Money for what?"

"He gave me his textbook the last time I came here and I haven't paid."

She huffed and shook her head. "Why are you lying? He does not give any student textbook before they pay."

The clock in her office chimed. I looked at the phone in my hands to see that it was 2:00 P.M. I remembered the twins in day care, calculated how long it would take me to get to them, considering that most schools would be closing soon and that meant traffic jam. I decided then that trying to convince a secretary who guarded her boss's office like a lair was not worth it.

"Ok. I'll wait till I see him in class." I moved to the door then waited, looking at her to leave so I could pass through. She didn't seem in a hurry to have me leave anymore.

Lazily she pushed away from the door and stretched out her hand, "So where is the money?"

"Please make sure he gets it." I counted the money out of my purse, but did not fail to notice the wounded expression she was wearing. "It's just that he may not remember so if you can write my name and what I'm paying for I think it will help." I tried to explain.

"I know my job," she tossed back heading for her desk. She sat, waited a moment then looked up at me. "What are you still waiting for?"

"For you to write my name down somewhere."

She shook her head, looking exasperated, then without another word went back to her typing. After standing for almost a minute and finally coming to the realisation that she was ignoring me, I took out a paper and pen from my bag, wrote my name, department, and the amount of money, then handed it to her. When she refused to collect it from me, I placed it on her desk and left to join Kosi.

We were nearing Kosi's hostel so I could collect some more of her notes to update mine when she broke the silence to ask what had happened between Abike and me.

"You don't want to be in her black book," Kosi warned after I told her everything that happened from the first day when I came to see Professor Okoro, though I left out my reason for coming to see him. "She has influence in this department based on what I've heard our senior colleagues say. If she doesn't like you, she will make sure you get into trouble with Professor Okoro." She looked around then lowered her voice considerably. "They said people who have stepped on her toes end up having missing scripts in Okoro's course." Her forefinger went to her mouth and her eyes darted about again. "I didn't tell you anything o." She pulled at her ear for emphasis.

"Wait. Is it that she removes the person's exam script by herself or she is close to Okoro enough to influence him not to release someone's result?" I had to know.

She hit the back of her right hand against her left palm then did the same with the back of her left hand on her right palm, before opening both hands, palms facing upwards. "My dear, I don't know o. I'm just telling you what I heard."

Before I could process this new bit of information, she stopped and nudged me with her elbow in my ribs. I looked at her, then followed the direction of her gaze to where they settled. I felt my heart jump, the way fireworks shoot straight into the sky before exploding into hammering heartbeats, so violently I feared my chest would burst open. He was just too gorgeous, my Obinna, I thought painfully. Perhaps, if he was not, it would be easier to stay angry with him. He was standing with a group of boys, four of them, laughing. It was hard not to be drawn in by his laughter. He was not the tallest in the group, but what he lacked in height he more than made up for in build and charisma.

Upon noticing my anger was starting to slip away, I made an effort to remember the events of the previous night and especially the words he used that stung so much. That brought back the resentment and I held on to it like a weapon against his charm, using it to drag my eyes away from him and get my feet to move. Before I could go far, I heard a loud greeting and instinctively knew it was directed at me though there were lots of people around. I debated with myself whether to stop and acknowledge the greeting, or pretend I didn't hear it and get on my way, when I heard, "Mummy twins." I stopped, not sure how to react. It was just who I had expected it to be: Kanu. His huge grin discouraged me from responding negatively. Keeping a straight face, I acknowledged his greeting with a nod and was about to keep moving when he signalled for me to join them. Obinna's eyes and mine met and held. I saw the warning in them before he turned back to his friends, turning Kanu's face away from me as he did.

"What's his problem?" Kosi asked, eyeing Obinna's back and dragging me with her, away from them.

"I don't know," I answered, thinking back to past events and wondering if it was just the event of the previous night or there was something else that happened to warrant such animosity.

"Hah! Boys ehn." She let out a long hiss. We were already at the entrance to her hostel, Moremi hall. "Once they get what they want they will turn to monsters. In fact they are all monsters pretending to be nice just to have their way." I looked at her now wondering if she was still referring to my case or something more personal. It was on the tip of my tongue to ask her what boys had done to her, but I decided against it, knowing I did not have the time to wait to listen if she chose to share.

"Go and bring the note, I'll wait here for you," I said instead.

"Don't you want to come in?"

"Uh uh. I can't. I'm already late to pick them from day care."

Chapter Nine

*I*t was a normal thing for me to sit and wallow in regret at the wrong turns I had taken in my life. I was doing it again and it made me feel extremely miserable as I trudged under the weight of two children who were getting weightier by the day. Sweat from my hair made a path through my brow, down my chin and neck to be finally absorbed by the yellow *kilikili* star wrapper I used to secure Chuka to my back. I rocked a fussy Chika in my arm and patted her back to pacify her. Sweat, tears and saliva dripped from her face to mix with the wetness on my shoulder. Nothing I did would appease her and I feared her brother would wake to join her. One could hardly blame her for squirming, what with the sun shining down mercilessly. I would probably cry were I not an adult. As a matter of fact, I was already close to tears. To avoid that, I started singing to her. The song came out in breathless gasps, distorting the melody.

My chest ached, as did my limbs. The straps of two bags - my handbag and the large bag containing the children's things- bit painfully into the skin of my shoulder. I imagined my ancestors returning from the farm, bearing their farm produce, trekking miles to their homes; I imagined they could not have felt worse than I was feeling.

An Okada sped past, the rider whistling to get my attention. I longed to stop him and be driven home. That longing was quenched instantly. I knew better than to go against my parents' counsel and mount a bike with the babies. Someone who knows them could see me and report to them. Unfortunately, I could not afford to take a taxi. I had stopped one at Enitan Street, where the day care was located, and could not understand the reason for his expensive fare. It was only a five-minute ride. After trying five cab drivers, all with similar rates, I chose to trek rather than endure more insults from foul-mouthed drivers.

Usually, I took a bus when going home with the kids. It was the cheapest and was safer than a bike, though that meant stopping at the bus stop to trek down two streets before getting home. But, on this day, there were no buses on the road due to a strike by the Nigerian Union of Road Transport Workers.

Chika's wail grew louder, calling attention to us. I heard the side comments as we passed a mechanic workshop.

See her, small girl like this don born pikin.

No. Dem no fit be her pikin.

Na she get them, I sabi am when she carry the belle.

I kept my eyes down on the tarred road and concentrated on counting my breath. Now more than ever, I realised the lack of wisdom in my actions those months ago. Resentment bubbled at having to suffer the consequences alone and it threatened to spill out. I had a strong urge to stop by the side of the road, sit there with the babies and scream at the injustice. Obinna was meant to be with me, holding one of the children. It was only right. Instead he was in school, probably having fun with his friends at my expense and telling them how easy I had been. I agonised over the possibility of that thought.

Unable to endure the pain in my chest, I stopped in front of a kiosk by the side of the road and dropped the bags on the floor. Tomato juice dripped from large baskets of tomatoes placed on a table and pooled on the bench below. I eased onto the small dry spot on the bench and laid Chika on my lap.

"Wetin you wan buy, fine customer?" A woman called from inside the wooden stall.

"Nothing," I answered, opening the bag on the floor to search through it.

"Why you come dey block market for me? Leave my shop jare." The switch in her tone was quick. My hand found the feeding bottle and pulled it out, just as I heard her footstep coming out of the stall toward me. The bottle was empty.

Before seeing her, I knew she would be overweight. The planks on which her stall was built shook as she walked across them to stand in front of me, arms akimbo. Her *buba* went round her waist only once and looked like it would come undone from its stingy knot if she moved too much. I had an impression the hands on her waist were there to keep the wrapper from falling.

Prepared to butter her up so she would allow me a minute to console my crying child, I greeted her in what limited Yoruba I could speak. From experience, I knew Yoruba women like it when someone speaks their language to them, but this woman ignored my greeting and frowned down at Chika.

"You no see say hunger dey wire this pikin? Feed am jare," she ordered.

I raised the empty feeding bottle, hoping that would be a satisfying answer.

"Wetin be that? Na that bottle be the breast wey God give you?" With no respect for personal space, she bent and loosened the wrapper tied round my chest, grabbed both wrapper and a still sleeping Chuka, then forced open my zip in one quick, crude move. Her eyes dared me to protest. However, seeing the way she was hugging Chuka to her ample bosom, I felt more grateful than angry. Painfully aware of the people passing by in the street, I tried to close the zip, but she was faster and slapped my hand off.

"Wetin you dey do? You want make I help you comot am?" She bent toward me again and I shook my head, stole a quick glance around, before pulling my blouse up, just a little. I placed Chika's head under my blouse. She latched on quickly and began to suckle.

I looked up to see the woman frowning at me. What again?

"How she go take breathe? Arrange your pikin well. Wetin you dey hide?" She asked.

"But she is no more crying, mummy," I silently pleaded for understanding.

She needled me with her eyes, her mouth bent at the corners to express her disapproval, but said nothing more. She went inside with Chuka to sort tomatoes.

Silence reigned as Chika nursed until I heard a familiar voice call my name. I looked up into Kingsley's surprised face. I was surprised as well because I expected him to have left for school, not be in Lagos. Quickly, I pulled Chika away from my breast and pulled the blouse all the way down. Ignoring the piercing howl she let out, I fumbled as I worked my zip.

By the time I was done, he was already at the stall, standing in front of me and talking a little too excitedly, obviously to mask his discomfort at the position he found me in. As I returned his greeting, I noticed his eyes journey to my chest then dart off immediately, and I looked down to see a wet patch steadily growing from a tiny drop to a large map on my chest. I held my breath, with the hope that the milk flow would ebb, but it was useless. Unable to meet his eyes again, I directed every effort into comforting Chika.

"What are you doing here?" he asked, still not looking at my face.

"What are you doing here too? Shouldn't you be in school?" He had told me at my party that he was leaving for the University of Calabar the following day and I didn't expect to see him in Lagos one week later.

"I will leave this weekend," he answered then repeated his previous question to me.

"I'm just coming back from school and stopped to pick them from day care. I'm on my way home now." To cover the wetness on my chest, I lifted Chika and carried her at chest level.

"Only you? Carrying both of them?" He looked incredulous. I nodded and despite myself chuckled at his shock.

"Why didn't you take a taxi or something?"

I conveniently ignored his question and zipped the maternity bag at my feet. The tomato seller came forward then, eyed me and curved her lips downwards in distaste. I bent my head in shame. I knew she was disappointed in me. What mother will stop a hungry baby from suckling mid-meal simply because she was embarrassed? I was ashamed of my behaviour but was still uncomfortable about baring my breast in the presence of an audience, worse in the presence of a former love interest.

I dismissed the guilt with a shake of my head. Just this once, I consoled myself, and she will never see me again to lay those judgemental eyes on me. Balancing Chika on one hip, I reached out my hand to collect Chuka, who had woken up, from her. Kingsley reached him before I could and with surprising deftness held the child with practised hands.

The thought of being seen by my mates with a baby tied to my back was a constant source of panic. That was something mothers did, not young girls, and doing that made me aware of a reality which I sometimes wanted to ignore. In the past, whenever I dreamt of being a mother, I imagined owning a car to drive wherever I wanted with a nanny tagging along to help with the baby, but my life turned out differently. However, as I secured Chika to my back with a wrapper, I did not worry about being seen with a baby at my back. It was either that or the whole neighbourhood would see me in a shirt soaked with breast milk.

With Chika secured, I reached down for the bags and found only my handbag there. Kingsley was with the other, searching through it.

"What are you looking for?"

"Is it only one wrapper you have here?" He frowned looking into the bag, supporting Chuka with one hand and digging in the bag with the other.

"Wait. Are you trying to back him?" I doubled over laughing.

"You think I can't?" The look on his face was a dare. I imagined him with a baby tied to his back. It was an out-of-place image and caused fresh laughter to shake my body.

"I know you can," I agreed, holding up my free hand. "But please don't." To keep from laughing more, I pressed my lips together tightly and tried to keep a straight face. "Have you ever seen any man with a baby on his back?"

He considered this momentarily then burst out laughing too.

After thanking the owner of the stall, we started off down Brown Road, in the direction that led to my street; he with Chuka and the maternity bag; I, carrying Chika and my hand bag. This is what a couple should be like, I found myself thinking, then held my thought as soon as I noticed it leaning toward regret.

Saturdays were never my best days, mainly because I loved school days when I was in secondary school and also because I hated chores—and Saturdays were for chores. But when the weekend came at the end of the second week of my life as a university student, I welcomed it like a child would a mother just back from work.

It was satisfying to spend extra hours in bed. It seemed even the twins were happy not to be roused from sleep so early and they slept for longer than usual, waking only after I had had my fill of rest.

Feeling stronger and in better spirits, I stood in front of the gas cooker, stirring the blended tomatoes simmering on the fire and telling an attentive Nnenna what university life was like. I was barely done answering one question before she was out with another.

"So, nothing like flogging there, ehn?" She asked with wide, eager eyes. She was kneeling on a kitchen stool as she leaned over the kitchen counter. Her elbow rested on the Formica countertop so that she could support her chin with her hand.

"Flog for what? Who has that time?"

"Yes!" She said triumphantly, pumping her left fist in the air. "Ah. Can't wait to leave secondary school and outlive flogging."

"Don't be so happy yet o. They may not flog you, but what they do to you is worse than flogging."

"Nothing can ever be worse than flogging. Turn that tomato well o. I can smell it burning. Do anything to me, but just don't bring cane near me."

"That's what you think until you get there and meet very intimidating lecturers that will make you want to pee on yourself just by looking at you." I turned the burner to lower the heat and continued to stir, scraping the bottom of the pot where the tomato was sticking.

She shook her head in refusal. "It is still better than flogging. Looks don't hurt, cane does."

"But failing you can hurt."

"They can't fail me if I write well in exams."

"Yes they can, in fact, they do."

She eyed me and gave a single nod of disbelief.

"You think I'm lying? A lecturer can seize your result, or cause you to have a missing script. Besides, it is not like secondary school where you see your exam script after they've marked it. Once you've submitted, that's it, no more. So even if you like write heaven and earth, if the lecturer doesn't like you he can give you an F and there's nothing you can do about it."

"Ahn ahn. For what naa? I will report." She pushed away from the countertop and knelt upright, already bristling.

"Who do you want to report to?"

"Anybody. His superior, maybe."

"It doesn't happen that way. Report one lecturer and every lecturer will gang up against you, so just forget about graduating."

That got her attention and she frowned, shaking her head as if to get rid of what she just heard. I knew she was bound to launch into a rant about how wrong that was, but before she could do so, we heard Obinna's voice. My hand froze mid-stir while she dropped her feet to the floor and stood, alert.

"Continue turning this." I handed the spoon to Nnenna, impulsively finger-combed my hair and assessed my reflection on the shiny surface of the stainless steel pot. That elicited a snort from Nnenna which I ignored and started out of the kitchen.

Almost to the door, I heard him say, "I want to see them" and I raced through the door before any of my sisters would let him.

"No, you can't see them." I jumped in front of him before he could take a step further. He sighed tiredly and looked away, obviously exasperated at having to deal with me, then he looked back at me.

"You can't keep me from seeing my own children," he said with emphasis on the last word.

"So now you refer to them as 'my own children'?" I asked, mimicking his voice. "When you were denying them in front of your friends you didn't know, ehn? Now you want to claim father. Come and claim let me see you." I turned to the door that led into the rooms and, gently nudging Ujunwa through, I locked it and removed the key, holding it tight as if I expected him to struggle for it.

"What is wrong with you Ada?"

"The same thing that was wrong with you when you denied your own children." I threw back, finally satisfied at having an outlet for the anger I had held on to for the whole week.

"I never denied my children. What has come over you?"

"The same thing that came over you when you saw me in school and pretended you didn't know me. Please stop standing there pretending to be innocent. You refused to admit that you have children when people were around, now you want to come and play at being a father in secret? No, that's not how it works. You are either a parent or you are not. No middle ground."

"Fine. I'm a parent. Now can I see them?" he stretched out his hand for the key.

"No. Being a parent is more than saying it with your mouth. It is about taking responsibility for them even when it doesn't suit you. Unfortunately, instead of you to be the one volunteering to help out with the kids and making enquiry about them, you are not. Most people would think it is Kingsley who is their father with the way he cares for them."

I was still talking and didn't notice the change in his countenance. I had expected him to talk back and when he didn't I searched his face and noticed the boy before me had gone rigid. But for the strain in his cheek, resulting from a strongly clenched jaw, one would have thought it was a statue in front of me. He was perfectly still but his eyes blazed and his nose flared dangerously.

His eyes bore into mine. My skin itched and I suddenly felt hot. I had a strong urge to scratch under my armpits, but controlled it and returned his gaze with as much challenge as I could infuse in mine. When his body finally began to move, it was not reassuring like I thought it would be. His fists clenched by his sides and he raised them. I eyed them, a part of me certain he would never try to use his fists on me, yet I was not sure I knew the boy I was staring at or what he was capable of anymore. He brought both fists to his front, then smacked them together. The cracking sound caused me to flinch and brought Nnenna running out of the kitchen. She stood looking at us for a moment, before she came to me, searching my face.

"Did he hit you?" She asked, her hands touching me all over. I shook my head. She pried the keys out of my hand then stood before the door, like a sentry, eyeing Obinna and saying nothing else.

"What is Kingsley doing with my children?" He asked the question slowly, spacing each word out.

"What you wouldn't do with them." I returned calmly. The fight had gone out of me and I considered taking the key from Nnenna and letting him through, but I knew no one was going past that slim body with a resolve of steel, not even I, the sister she respects so much.

"Ada, I don't want him near them again."

Looking at him reminded me of a stormy weather, one that had just finished raging and seemed under control, but was actually brewing, waiting to come crashing anytime. I was not fooled by the calmness he was projecting, but I was determined not to let that keep me from speaking my mind.

"Obinna, if I need help with them and he offers to help me I will not refuse."

"Fine. If you need help with them call me," he tossed out carelessly.

"No, I wouldn't," I said and he narrowed those eyes at me. "I've never had to call Kingsley. He does so without being asked. I won't run after you to fulfil your duties."

"Maybe I will better fulfil my duties if you won't keep standing as a barrier between me and them. I'm here now to do just that, but you won't let me. It's their baptism next week. If you won't let me see them, at least tell me what plans you've made and what is left to be done."

I huffed out a breath and shook my head. "It's their baptism next week and not once all the while have you asked how you can pitch in, and you come in just some days to go asking how you can help. Did you think we were going to leave everything waiting until you were ready to offer your assistance? Sorry to disappoint you, Obinna, but we have sorted everything out. I'm even surprised you remembered."

"I won't let you make me feel like the worst father on earth."

"You don't need my help to do that. You've achieved it all on your own. I need to get back to cooking Obinna." I turned and started towards the kitchen then felt his hand clamp around my arm tightly. Nnenna started humming; it was more a warning than a melody, reminding Obinna of her presence. He released my arm but I didn't continue my retreat, instead, I turned and looked at him with raised brows.

"I need to see them," he pleaded.

I said nothing, just continued looking at him coolly. That must have angered him because he let go of what reins he had on his temper and shouted, "Will you stop being so stubborn and let me see my children?"

I ignored him and went into the kitchen, coming out only after I heard him stomp out of the house and bang the door after him.

Feeling completely drained, I lay on the couch and raised unseeing eyes to the ceiling.

"God knows I'll never get married." Nnenna pushed away from the door and came to stand behind the chair I occupied. "I will never let any man have that power over me to talk to me anyhow and treat me anyhow. What nonsense." Her hiss was long and shrill.

I fought the urge to protect my ears from them.

"I am not married," I reminded her.

"Well you are almost married, half way there."

"Which one is almost married? It's either you are married or you are not."

"Ok. You are not married," she allowed. "Yet you have to endure all the things married women suffer; a man thinking he owns you, talking to you anyhow and trying to run your life, no freedom."

"I still have my freedom hundred percent," I snapped at her. I was angry because the truth in her words stung. I was not so free anymore.

Unfazed by my mood, she continued, "Fifty percent maybe, but he owns you since you both share the same children. He will keep being a part of your life, whether you want him there or not. That is not total freedom. Total freedom is what I will have."

"Wait." It was important to me to clear things up. "Since we share the same children why then should he be the one who owns me? If that is the case, we own each other."

This elicited a sudden, loud bark of laughter from Nnenna. When she finally stopped rolling her head and her wheezing gradually quieted, she wiped the tears from her eyes.

"In what way do you own him? He does as he likes. You are the one who is stuck, Ada. Not him. It is you who have sleepless nights, who can't stay back after school and make new friends, who can't live a normal life, and it is just not fair!" Her sudden change of mood from amusement to indignation stunned me.

She shook her head vigorously and stared into the distance.

"Nobody will treat me that way. Nobody," she repeated emphatically. "And you shouldn't let anybody treat you like that too." She bent and looked down at me with wise eyes. "Stop it now before it is too late.

If he will not take equal responsibility then he doesn't deserve equal benefits."

"I thought you liked Obinna?"

"That was before. Children like everyone."

"Even until last year you still thought he was the best."

"That was before he got you pregnant and started misbehaving."

I felt a sudden need to defend Obinna. "Well it's not his fault. Some people find it harder adapting to parenthood."

"Look at you making excuses for him." She turned away from the chair and I heard the key move in the lock. "That's how it starts."

"Remind me how old you are again?"

"Fourteen going on forty," she answered, the cadence of her voice indicating that she was already in the corridor leading to the rooms.

Chapter Ten

The weekend was over before I had had enough of it. On Monday morning, as I walked along the corridor that led into my class and looked inside, my narrowed eyes had absolutely nothing to do with the harmattan wind blowing and raising brown clouds of dust that finally settled on every surface. It was shock and my reflection on one of the windows showed it. I avoided the impulse to look at the top of the door to confirm from the tag that I was in the right place.

As I walked into the room, everything indicated it was my class. The faces, now familiar after one week, were same. My class was exactly as I remembered it: a couple of glass panes missing from the jalousie window, numerous posters pasted on the notice board at the back of the class — some announcing free tutorials, others had hopeful faces, wearing cajoling smiles, asking for the students' votes — a ceiling fan with one blade missing; all that remained, but that was where the similarity ended.

The behaviour of my course mates did not add up and I found myself walking stealthily so my shoes would make minimal noise, in tune with the unusual quiet I had walked into. A brief survey of the class showed where Kosi was and I tiptoed there to take my place beside her.

On the tables, rather than students perching as was the norm, textbooks were laid out with heads bent towards them. My greeting to Kosi was returned with a nod.

"What is going on?" Finally unable to put it together myself, I asked Kosi in a whisper, but in the silence it came out loud, enough to cause a couple of heads to frown in my direction.

Kosi scribbled on a paper and pushed it to me: *Prof. Okoro's lecture now.*

For some reason, that alone made sense. My face was above my copy of *Introduction to Economics* when I felt, rather than saw, Professor Okoro walk in. The class grew quieter. I had no idea that was possible, but it did and a chill that I could not credit to the weather passed through me. When I looked up, eyes that, no doubt, missed nothing were scanning the class. I wondered why he looked so angry. He looked more frightening than I remembered from our last encounter.

"Good morning class," he greeted and, without waiting for the timid reply from the students to run its course, delved into explaining Devaluation.

It was my first time sitting through his lecture. He had been away the previous week and a junior lecturer had taken his course. As his distinct voice boomed through the fearsome silence and he explained currencies—how they were valued, on what occasions they lost value, and factors that could warrant devaluation—I was drawn in by his teaching style and was glad to have him teach me.

I scribbled fast, mostly in shorthand, to keep up with his incisive analysis. The topics which had seemed like jargon, impossible to understand when I studied the textbook privately, began to make sense. Briefly, I wondered why students disliked him and his lectures. While I could understand the dislike for him on a personal level, I could not comprehend why anyone would find fault with his method of teaching. Of all the lectures I had sat through the past one week, none came close to being as explanatory as his. I was already projecting towards the exam period and the time when I would break the record to become his first student to have an A or B. I would surprise him. Perhaps he'd be highly proud of me and be further convinced he had made the right choice by helping with my admission. I was determined to make that happen.

Riding on that determination, I heartily answered *"yes sir"* when he asked if he was making himself clear, then raised a hand to ask a question. I tensed upon realizing no one else had replied to his question. His eyes mirrored the surprise in the eyes of my course mates as they settled on me, then narrowed in recognition.

"You?" It was the shortest accusation I ever heard, the most confusing too, because I could not understand what I had done wrong or why I felt guilty and unsure.

"Good morning sir," was all I could manage and I struggled to maintain eye contact that was neither disrespectful nor cowardly as the silence stretched.

Just when I was about to bend my head to avoid looking into his scowling face, he closed the distance between us and bent at the waist to my level.

"Did you think you could escape or that I will not recognize you?"

"No sir."

"Or you think I will forget?"

"No Sir. I'm sorry sir," I apologised though I didn't know what for. I was aware that curious stares were cast my way, but it paled compared to Okoro's accusatory glare.

"I'm sorry sir, but I don't know what I have done wrong."

At this, he stood straight and angled his head as if insulted. I began shaking my head in denial and apology.

"You don't know what you've done wrong?" He waited and scolded when I did not answer. "You better answer me when I speak to you. Can't you talk?"

I swallowed to dislodge the barrier in my throat. "No sir... Yes, sir... I mean... Yes, I can talk, but, no, I don't know what I have done."

"You owe me money," I heard the intake of breaths that greeted his revelation and the embarrassment that washed over me pushed away what fear I felt. "When were you planning to pay?"

"But sir I've paid." My protest came out stronger than I intended.

"You dare talk back at me?"

"No Sir. Sorry, sir. It's just that… I paid to your secretary last two weeks Friday. I specifically told her it was the money for your textbook." I raised my voice as I said the last part so the rest of the class would hear it and know I was not involved in anything incriminating.

"I will sort it out with her today sir. I'm very sorry." My feet tapped rhythmically against the floor and I rocked myself to hold back the strong urge to pee. My eyes closed in relief when he turned away from me to walk back to the front of the class.

"Make sure you clear it with her before today is over," he ordered quietly and resumed teaching about the most valued currencies in the world, as naturally as if he had not just almost caused me to embarrass myself irrevocably by emptying my bladder there in full glare of everyone.

It was not until three hours past midday that I had a break from the day's lectures and was able to make it to Professor Okoro's office. I hoped not to meet him and was relieved when Abike informed me that he was away.

Abike was at the far right side of her office, opposite the door, when I walked in. She was squatting in front of a steel file cabinet and barely spared me a glance after she turned to see who it was, informed me that the Professor was not on seat, then returned her attention to the stack of files extending higher than her crouched figure.

"It is you I came to see." I folded my arm across my chest and prepared for a confrontation. She said nothing and continued to open, fill, and close drawers. I noticed she got her hair braided. The braids extended to her waist. Prior to that day, I had only ever seen her wearing her natural hair, held back with a hair band. Her clothes were also different from her usual secretary outfit of crispy, starched, cotton shirt and dark skirt made from thick material. She was wearing a yellow chiffon blouse tucked into a navy blue pencil skirt that hugged her curvy backside and was cinched at the waist with a wide tummy belt. Her buttocks seemed larger and the extra roundness, I attributed to her bent position.

"Why didn't you give Professor Okoro the money I paid you for his textbook?"

She ignored me and with each second that passed, the reins on my temper loosened. I considered and dismissed several courses of actions to take. Before I could decide on one, she spoke calmly.

"How can you prove that you gave me any money?" she asked me but her eyes stayed on the files she was sorting.

My heart began to thunder as the implication of her words registered. "I gave you one thousand five hundred Naira last two weeks Friday, Abike. Or are you going to deny that?"

"Except you have proof, it will be your word against mine." Her dismissive tone added anger to the fear I was trying to hold down. I knew I was treading on a thin, dangerous line. Wondering on the best way to handle the situation and afraid of how she would react in return, I chose to stay calm. My head shaking in denial was the only part of my body in motion.

"I wrote my name down for you on a piece of paper," I tried again.

"Produce the paper then and show me my signature on it showing that I accepted money from you."

I stomped to the front of the cabinet so she would have no choice but to look at me. I needed to see her face too.

"What is the meaning of this? Move away from my front," she said. She lifted her head then and I noticed the difference was not only in her attire. She had makeup on, not the quickly drawn or simplistic job of an amateur, but expertly drawn eyebrows, long, dark lashes and lips that looked like an oiled red apple. Her eyelids shimmered with bronze eye shadow. I never imagined I would think of Abike as beautiful but I did then. She looked nothing like herself and everything like a face from a glossy glamour magazine, although the stinky behaviour remained and that kept me from voicing the compliment that was at the tip of my tongue.

She stood languorously. The wedge sandals she had on made her taller. At her full height, I had to raise my eyes to meet hers. Those eyes gave me a baleful look and I thought the expression and the face did not match. Perhaps it would work on a face like Professor Okoro's, not hers, then I reminded myself that the face was only a mask, a beautiful one, hiding a dark personality bent on making my life miserable.

"What do you have against me, Abike?"

She snorted. "You think I have time for you, let alone to have anything against you?" She gestured for me to move. "Leave there let me do my work."

Instinctively, I opened my mouth to voice my outrage, but, realizing that would not help my case, I changed tactics.

"Abike, I beg you now, please don't let me get into trouble with Professor Okoro."

She looked at me long and hard but I could see that she was already reconsidering and I held my breath.

"Go and sit down. I'll attend to you when I finish this." She gestured to the files on the floor between us.

I sat in silence, watching her work, then got bored and began to play Snake Xenzia on my phone, making sure to put off the volume. After having my snake head hit against the obstacle and losing my life several times, I got bored with that too and became impatient as the hand counting the seconds on my wristwatch circled.

I contemplated begging her to halt her job and attend to me but knew she would not understand my hurry. I stood and paced to the door and back hoping she would get the message. When that didn't work, I sat and tapped my palm against the arm of the chair repeatedly, huffed, hissed softly and snapped my fingers. Everything I did to get her attention either went unnoticed or was intentionally ignored. The files were not diminishing fast enough and when I could not stand it any longer, I went to stand beside her by the cabinet.

"Can I help you with this so we can be faster?" I held my breath after asking, fearing she would take it the wrong way, and she did.

"Are you trying to tell me that I'm wasting your time?"

"Nooo. No that's not what I'm saying oh." I raised my hand innocently. "It's just that I'm in a hurry."

"You are always in a hurry. Do you have children that you're taking care of?"

"Yes." The truth came out before I could think, causing her hand to stiffen on the drawer she was about closing. She looked at me, surprise and disbelief clearly etched on her face, then her eyes moved to my left hand.

I knew what she was expecting to see. The world was not accepting of unwed mothers and Nigerians especially were known to be very critical of such women. I knew too well the stigmatization that could result from disclosing my single mother status, so I lied.

"I don't wear my ring. But I have two children." I could not explain why it was important for me that she believed me, especially when I was trying so hard to keep that part of my life private. "I need to go pick them from day care and I'm late already."

She turned away from her task to give me her full attention. "So you really have children? No wonder."

"No wonder what?"

She shrugged as if her meaning should be clear enough. "You know, you don't act like a fresher. You come in here, not afraid, talking to me as if we are mates. Now I understand why. You probably are older than me."

Rather than tell her I was only sixteen, I decided to act as mature as she assumed me to be. I widened my eyes a bit and looked her square in the face, the way a senior would a junior. Her eyes lowered slightly in respect, a rare smile playing on her lips. She abandoned the files stacked on the floor and motioned for me to follow her as she went to her desk.

The notebook she brought out was long with a hard cover. I collected the pen she passed to me and pulled the opened book closer to myself.

"Write your name here," she pointed as she spoke, "your department here, level, what you are paying for, amount, then sign here." I did all that and when I was done she turned the book to herself and signed.

She shook her head when her eyes met mine again.

"It will be really hard for you o, combining schooling and being a mother. You should have done the part time program, that way you'll come to school only on weekends and holidays. That's what most people with children do. In fact, you are the first regular student I've met who is a mother from her first year. The few who try combining regular studies and parenting start having kids either in third year or final year. Still it always affects their results. I just wonder how you will cope."

She raised her right elbow to the table and rested her chin on her palm, her eyes were sympathetic. "Just try your best and see if you can graduate with at least a second class lower, you hear?"

With great effort, I clamped down on the instinct to openly rebuke her words. I could see she sincerely thought she was wishing me the best attainable considering my circumstance, so I let it go.

"So is this all I have to do to see that this thing is sorted with Prof?" I stood and looked meaningfully at my wrist watch.

"Yes. That will be all. You can go now." Her smile now came too easily and often.

Feeling generous, I finally gave her the compliment I had held in.

"You are looking very fine today oh. Your hair, your clothes, even your make up. You should be looking like this every day."

Her face lit up considerably while her palm smoothed the neat braids. "Today is my birthday o, so I decided to do something extra. I'm twenty-two today."

"Wow! Happy birthday, dear. You really are young o." I shook my head, baffled. I had pinned her for someone in her late twenties or early thirties, probably due to her usually stern face and prim clothes, but in her beautiful dress and makeup it was easy to believe the age she claimed.

"I know, but shhh." She stood too and held her forefinger to her lips "Don't tell those your course mates before they start disrespecting me like I'm their mate."

I nodded my promise. "But birthday or not you should always look good like this. You look too sweet. Hope you've taken picture today?"

"Ah, yes, I have o. First thing I did as I entered school this morning was to stop at the picture stand."

"And after school?"

She angled her head, twisted her mouth to one side and managed to look forlorn "Nothing o."

"Ahh, don't let that fine dress waste o. Take yourself out or get somebody to take you out."

"Not all of us are as lucky as you with a husband who will take us out on our birthday."

"Why do you need someone to take you? Since you are working, take yourself and, who knows, while you are there you may meet somebody cute." I winked and she laughed heartily, clapping her hands.

"Ok o. I will try. *Oya,* go before you'll be late"

I took out one hundred Naira note from my handbag and pushed into her hand. "Buy malt for yourself and celebrate."

"Ahh. Thank you o. Thank you."

That was how I left the dean's office, with the usually fearsome Abike showering me with thanks and smiling respectfully.

Chapter Eleven

Making sacrifices and foregoing important things for other equally or more important ones came with the territory of motherhood and I was adapting quickly. The matriculation ceremony for new students kept being postponed and when the final date was fixed, it clashed with the day the twins were scheduled to be baptised. I did not think twice about where I would be on that day.

The baptism was a beautiful ceremony, one that was not diminished by the fact that my children were born out of wedlock. Despite being the only unmarried mother among the parents who brought their children to be baptised on the same day, my children, Obinna and I participated fully in the process involved in a typical Catholic infant baptism.

My entire family and Obinna's family were there too. Geoffrey, a male cousin of Obinna's stood in as Chika's godfather. Ama was her godmother and was patient enough to stay and fulfil the duties required of her new role before rushing off immediately after Mass to don her matriculation gown for the ceremony. Chuka's godparents were friends of Obinna's parents and total strangers to me, but they were accepting of the twins, and of me, so I had no problems with them, nor with the officiating priest who carried each of my children like they were infinitely precious – in or out of wedlock – while anointing their chests and foreheads lavishly with oil and pouring holy water on their heads.

Unfortunately, I could not enjoy that degree of acceptance everywhere.

One Friday morning, on the week after the baptism, as I trudged through the open gates of Coker-Aguda Primary Health Centre to face a responsibility I dreaded, I knew I had every reason to be nervous about being judged for my choices.

I had skipped my lectures for that day to take them for their sixteenth-week check-up and polio immunization, but I would have preferred to sit through Professor Okoro's lecture than have to deal with the overworked, underpaid, eternally irritated and impatient government-employed nurses.

A heavy weight settled in my chest, slowing my steps as I walked across the spacious car park to the open hall to drop my children's appointment cards into the basket provided for that purpose. Despite the cold, wet patches soaked through the underarms of my blouse. I remembered to bend at the knees as I greeted the two female hospital administrators seated at the registration bench and received from them a paper with numbers written on them: 67, 68.

Avoiding eye contact as best as I could, I made my way to the waiting area to take a seat with other patients. Chairs were arranged in two rows and I went to the last seat on the row closest to me.

"Are you the last person?" I asked one of the occupants.

"God forbid, I can never be the last person in Jesus name," the woman answered as she raised both arms and moved them in a circular motion; starting from the back of her head, over it, then to the front where she snapped the fingers of both hands. She did this multiple times.

Taking a deep breath, I made effort not to roll my eyes and tried again. "Are you the last person on the queue?"

"My friend, sit down anywhere you want and stop asking nonsense questions. Don't you know your number? When they call your number you'll go, ahn," another woman in the same seat said over her baby's head.

I gritted my teeth to keep from hissing and lowered myself into an available seat.

The queue moved slowly as the two nurses who weighed the babies took their time while chatting with each other. Movement was orderly. As soon as the mother next in line stood with her baby to go to the nurse for weighing, another would take her place, making space for those from the back bench to move forward. The line moved this way, with women sliding across benches and standing to move to the bench in front until it got to their turn.

As I sat awaiting my turn, I listened to the women exchanging mothering experiences. They talked about sleepless nights, habits their babies were picking up and progress being made, their babies' feeding patterns and the best formulae for babies. Harried mothers juggled crying babies on their thighs while some stood and paced with babies who would not be easily pacified.

One mother whose baby wouldn't stop crying no matter what she did swore this would be her last child.

"Indeed," another mother turned up her nose at her. "Just small petting from *oga* and you'll open your legs again." Most of the women laughed in agreement.

There were two men who accompanied their wives but they were silent, sometimes smiling, but never contributing.

"No way o," the mother who spoke earlier insisted. "I cannot go through this stress again. Three children are enough for me."

"OK o," another said sarcastically. "We shall see."

The chatter continued as did the cry of babies. The place had a mix of strong smells: milk, poo, urine from unchanged nappies and diapers, talcum powder, and the food the hospital planned to share to every mother. The meal for the day was porridge; I could see the huge stainless bowl sitting in front, beside the desk where the administrators sat and just behind the nurses weighing the babies.

Plastered on the walls were pictures with mother and child care tips. Nurses in fitted white shirts and matching white skirts or trousers darted in and out of the open doorway leading from the hall into the office area. The head nurse, Mrs Adeleke came out and the nurses weighing the babies quickened their pace.

Mrs Adeleke was a woman well revered by nurses, mothers, and younger doctors alike, so much so that it bordered on fear, and she seemed to relish the tension her presence elicited. Mothers bent at the knee to greet her, a greeting she barely acknowledged with a lift of her hand. She was an average-sized woman, but her backside was a different story. It looked like it had been cut out from a fat woman's body and attached to hers by a perverted plastic surgeon. It overstretched her white trousers and, as she walked, the pair rolled as if they would fall off any minute.

As the weighing continued under Mrs Adeleke's supervision, she delved into a lecture on mother and child care and hygiene. She scolded mothers with babies whose nappies were soiled or not white enough when they were stripped to be weighed. She also scolded a mother whose baby had catarrh running down her nose and into her mouth. Mothers adjusted themselves and their babies as they listened to her and I hoped that I would meet her approval when it got to my turn.

She was talking about child spacing and was condemning mothers who have toddlers and infants with less than two years gap between them and my heart beat increased when it neared my turn. I had advanced to the second seat when I looked toward the gate and saw Obinna strolling in, looking around uncertainly. We were still not talking. Though we managed to act civilized during the baptism, we did not talk to each other unless we had to, yet relief coursed through me when I sighted him.

He smiled when he noticed the arm I lifted to draw his attention and came over. One person moved forward to the front seat so he took the empty space and relieved me of both babies, refusing when I tried to hold on to one.

"Don't worry. You've been carrying them alone since, so I can too."

Mrs Adeleke glowered at us and I signalled for him to speak softly.

He frowned at the bowl of porridge a matron held in front of my face. When I shook my head in refusal she moved to the next person.

"Do they always share food?"

"Yes. Why did you come, Obinna?"

"I could say because I'm their father, but that wouldn't be the right answer and I know you will tell me that I knew I was their father yet I denied them." He bent his head for a while then looked back at me. "I came because you were right and I was wrong. I haven't been pulling my weight. I have left it all to you and I realize it isn't fair."

One mother stood and others slid along. Obinna stood and moved to the front seat so that we were separated momentarily, halting our conversation. When we moved again, I joined him then took Chika from him and began to remove her overall while he removed Chuka's. They had not stirred at all.

"So you always have to do this alone; get both of them out of their clothes and back into it?"

"Well, Kingsley has never been here to help me through this, if that's what you mean."

His face clouded over and he looked away.

"I do it alone and it's never easy. It's relatively simple today because they are sleeping and quiet. Usually, they are crying and kicking and I have to handle all that alone." I lifted an almost-naked Chika to my shoulder and he did same with Chuka. Only their diaper was on them, to be removed just before it was our turn, not sooner.

"I'm sorry," he said simply. He looked remorseful and my heart softened toward him. I reached for his free hand and squeezed.

"Won't you miss your lectures?"

"You are missing yours too, so..." he pointed out

"Well, I'm the one who was foolish enough to get pregnant, so I'm the one who has to deal with that."

He winced at my words and said, "I have to apologise for that too." He shook his head and puffed out air noisily. "I'm so ashamed of myself. I will really want to make this right, but I don't know how."

His hand reached out to rest on my knee and gave it a soft squeeze.

His eyes on mine were earnest and shone too bright. When he spoke, his voice shook a bit. "Tell me, how can I make it right?"

Before I could answer, my phone rang. It was from Kosi.

I pushed the green button as I held the phone to my ear then flinched immediately and put space between the phone and my ear. Even with my phone a few inches away, I could still hear Kosi's loud voice. The agitated tone had my heart beat increasing before I made out the implication of her words. I stood hurriedly with Chika nestled in my arm and darted across the hall without bothering to pick up the clothes that fell from my lap. Satisfied that I was a safe distance away from being a distraction to Mrs Adeleke and incurring her wrath, I gave my attention to Kosi's voice and picked the end of her ramblings.

"… so if you know what's good for you start coming now."

"Kosi, I'm very far away... still in Aguda. I don't know if I can make it." I shifted from one foot to the other. My bladder was suddenly so full it was painful holding it in.

"Ha. That's far o," she whispered then was silent for a while. I could imagine her considering various options. I thought of an option, started to voice it, then hesitated. I wasn't sure how she would handle it. I had only known her for a few weeks, not enough to gauge how my suggestion would affect how she viewed me. Then the predictions of Abike, that the best I could do, considering my responsibilities, was a second class lower, forced its way into my thoughts and that pushed me to try.

"Can you write for me?" The closest person was more than six feet away from me and could not hear me except they had a super sense of hearing, yet I whispered the abominable request.

"What?" Her reaction was not far from my expectation, but because I had hoped for a favourable answer her shocked reaction troubled me and I imagined covering her mouth with my palm to prevent her from repeating aloud what I had just said to her. I thought to ask her to ignore my request. That was what I was going to say to her when I started to speak, instead, I found myself pleading.

"Please Kosi. I have heard people do things like that. I can't make it in time." As I spoke I was getting more desperate. Chika started to whimper. "God, I can't make it. Who will I leave the babies for?" I pushed further hoping it would soften her.

"God! Ada, it's too dangerous. Me, I'm scared." Then, suddenly, she said, "Wait!" and my heart stopped its free dive to my feet and soared. "What if I call Ama to come in and sit on your behalf? She can copy from me."

Relief started from beneath my feet and ran up through my body in cold waves, like a cool breeze on a blistering afternoon.

"Yes!" Why didn't I think of that? "I'll call her now." I felt the need to salvage my image before Kosi and to apologise for expecting such from her, but I decided that would come later.

Time was doing the only thing it does best and I had to keep up. I cut the call and started to call Ama. While it rang, I caught sight of Obinna in the periphery of my vision trying to get my attention. I got back to him as he stood and moved with Chuka to the scale.

"Test," I replied to his questioning stare. His eyes widened with worry for me but I waved it away and smiled my reassurance. The smile was replaced with dread when Ama did not pick up. I tried again, and again it rang to the end. The nurse took Chuka from him and put him into the scale. Immediately, I thrust Chika into his arms and started to hurry to my bag but before I could go far, his hand shot out and held mine, stopping me.

"I have to go. We are having a test now and I don't want to miss it."

"I don't think you can make it Ada."

"Yes I can if I take a bike." I tried to pull my hand free but he held on.

"No way!" His expression and his tone brooked no argument, but I wasn't going to let him stop me. "I'm not letting you take a bike all the way to Akoka. It's too dangerous."

"I'm not going to let you make me miss my first test."

"It's just a test, Ada."

"No. It's more than just a test. It could be the difference between me graduating with a two-one and a two-two." His head jerked back in shock and his brows came together, forming concentration lines on his forehead and he looked at me like I had morphed into something he didn't know.

We were engaged in a tug of war, my arm being the rope, when Mrs Adeleke turned and drilled into us with her eyes. That caused his hand to slacken and I freed myself. They were done weighing Chuka and the nurse handed him to Obinna. Absently, Obinna collected Chuka and removed Chika's diaper, before handing her over to the nurse.

I suppressed the feeling of guilt, rattled off instructions to Obinna and flew through the gates, stopping the first bike I was lucky to see just outside the narrow street on which the health centre was situated. The bike rider was coated in reddish-brown dust, especially his eyebrows, lashes, and hair and I knew I would look very much the same after speeding through the express roads and street corners leading to the campus grounds.

I got to Aguda market before I realised I had not left anything for Obinna to feed the twins. I had not bothered to pump milk into their bottles because the source would be there with them all through the day, or so I had thought.

As the bike swallowed the distance and I warred with myself on whether to turn back or go on, I remembered I had not reminded him about collecting the hospital cards before leaving. Sweat trickled out of my palm, making me realize my fist was clenched. I opened it to find another reason to worry. I was holding the paper on which was written our numbers and had forgotten to give that to him too, yet I let the okada man continue his flight through the streets of Tejuosho and even tapped him on the back a few times to hurry him along.

It was not until after I was through with the test that I let myself feel again and the feelings came tumbling all at once: shame, disgust, fear, anger, guilt, disbelief. I could not believe I was capable of the things I had done.

Kosi tapped my shoulder. "Are you OK?"

I nodded as best as I could with my head bent on the table and my eyes to the ground. I knew I had to right the many wrong steps I had taken but was too weak to start. I was still catching my breath. The first step would be to apologise to Kosi for putting her in such compromising situation, then I had to hurry back to the hospital, no doubt with a bike again, and hope to make it in time before the kids became hungry or before Obinna got turned back from seeing the doctor because he did not have the papers on which the numbers were written.

I stiffened my body - I guess to block out all feelings and the hurt that could come from them - and lifted my head to look at Kosi.

"See… I hated to ask you to do something that would make you so uncomfortable." I began, only to have her look at me as though I had lost my mind.

"Babe, If I were in your shoes I would have done the same and even guilt-tripped you until you helped me."

My disbelief obviously showed on my face because she laughed and nudged my shoulder with hers. "For real. And I would have helped you, but I was afraid because I have not had time to study these lecturers to know how to outsmart them. Don't worry yourself jare. At least you still wrote the test," she assured me and as I prepared to leave, I hoped the second confrontation would go as smoothly as the first.

I was let into Obinna's home by a new face. She looked like the rest who came and went sooner than the lifespan of a bee; about the same age range - early to mid-teens - low cut hair and a timid demeanour.

I asked if Obinna was home and she looked at me, uncertainty and fear written all over her face.

"Please who are you?" she asked with an unsteady voice. I told her my name and asked again if Obinna was home.

"Wait, let me go and check," she said and went into the house after firmly locking the door.

I knew that meant Obinna was home but she needed to confirm from him if he wanted to see me. As I waited, I began to think back to all that had happened that day.

If death wanted me, that would have been a good day for it to take me. I had taken many risks and it wasn't even three o'clock yet. Asides taking a bike that sped above the limit of what is considered safe, I had also accepted a free ride from a total stranger in my haste to get home after I got to the hospital to find Obinna gone. It was not until I was in the strange man's car, listening to the heavily metallic songs blasting from the car stereo, exalting gangster life, gunshots, and death, that I began to worry for the first time that day. When my prayers were answered, and he dropped me off at home without incident, I promised to be more reasonable about my choices, especially when I had little ones depending on me.

They were not at my home either. Had I taken time to think, I would have known Obinna would not go there with them because he knew no one would be at my home at that time.

I felt sorry for the timid new house help who blocked my path as I started straight for Obinna's room after she returned to let me into the house. From the way she shifted her weight between both feet and the way her eyes darted between me and the door that led off into the living area, it was easy to see she was afraid; afraid to let me go straight into Obinna's room yet afraid of what would happen if she didn't let me in. Smiling easily, I patted her shoulder and told her she had nothing to fear.

I found Obinna on the floor, his body tilting from one side to the other, following the movement of his hands clutching a gamepad. Warmth spread through me at the sight, then he looked up and the guilt returned.

"Sorry." The single word sounded lame even to my ears. "I hurried back to the hospital but…" Noticing I was wringing my fingers, I folded my arm across my chest and braced for whatever would come.

He shrugged nonchalantly. "They attended to me earlier because they wouldn't stop crying." The *they* he was referring to were lying contented on his bed, making excited baby sounds.

"How did the test go? Did you meet up?" Game forgotten, Obinna put the pad aside and heaved himself up to the bed.

"Yes. Yes, I did eventually. He wouldn't let me in, but then I told him I was just coming from the hospital. Kosi confirmed my story so he finally let only me in."

"Thank God," he smiled, holding his hand out to me. I took it and joined him on the bed. We both looked down at the babies with smiles on our faces and at that moment I felt utterly content. Pushing away the regret that sprung at the thought that the beautiful picture we made was not permanent, I took in the sight and the feelings, storing them up for the future.

"Well, you just broke a record in the life of your children," I told him when my eyes met the pack of Caprisone on his bedside table.

"What?" He looked up anxious.

His eyes followed my hand as I gestured to the pack. "You are officially the first person to feed your children anything other than breast milk."

He cocked his head and smiled uncertainly. "Good or bad thing?"

"Well, you tell me. What was it like?"

His face exploded into a wide grin. "You should have seen them. They absolutely loved it. Chuka refused to let go of the straw even after his own finished. I had to give him some from hers," he relayed excitedly. "After this, I doubt if they'll ever want to settle for breast milk again."

"Hmmm. I won't be the one to suffer for that. Better get ready to buy cartons of Caprisone then."

"No problem."

"I just want them to have the best. They say six months exclusive breastfeeding is the best for babies so, for that reason, I hope you haven't put them off breast milk entirely."

I picked one of the packs and sucked noisily at the remaining drops.

"Come to think of it, this is the first time you are feeding them and I didn't get to watch. Talk about missed opportunities."

"Speaking of missed opportunities, I've never watched you breast-feeding them." His eyes on mine were heavy with desire and his voice lowered considerably, causing me to break out in goose bumps. "I'll love to watch you feed them," he said tenderly then reached for my hand and began caressing the fingers. Our eyes locked.

"I don't like breastfeeding in front of people." I looked away from those eyes that were already making me consider all sorts of forbidden things. "It makes me uncomfortable."

His hand cradled my chin and turned my face back, speaking only when my eyes looked into his. "I'm not people, Ada."

I was afraid to take that step. For some reason it felt like a huge step, silly it might seem considering all the steps we had gone through to get to this stage of becoming parents together, yet I needed an extra push to overcome the discomfort I was feeling at that point.

Soon he was handing Chuka to me. "I bet you Chuka will no longer rush for your milk like you say he does." There was challenge in his voice and his eyes twinkled with it.

"Never!" I received Chuka from him and before I could think or be overcome by the temporary immobility usually brought on by shyness, Chuka was already latched on and suckling greedily. I looked up to gloat and my breath caught in my chest. Never had anyone looked at me the way Obinna was doing at that moment. Words were useless. The utmost tenderness in his eyes made me feel like the world had shrunk and only the four of us were in it.

Wonder was clearly etched in his face and it was also evident in his voice when he spoke. "You make the best picture in the world."

Carefully, he lifted Chika and, placing her in his lap, he closed the space between us to rest his forehead on mine and link our fingers together.

A couple of hours later, much longer than I had planned, I was still with Obinna, both of us lying in the prone position on his bed, the twins snoozing between us. Pushing against the edges of my mind was the warning that his parents would be back soon. His mother, who was big on keeping promises, would not hesitate to let us know, in her silently disapproving manner, how disappointed she was that we had broken our pledge to keep away from each other when there was no one present to supervise.

"I should leave now," I said for the umpteenth time, yet made no move to rise from my position on the bed.

"Why?"

"It's getting late. Your parents will be back soon."

"I finally got a job," he blurted.

My gaze shifted from the ceiling to his face, my eyes questioning. I thought he had given up on that quest.

"One of the companies I applied to got back to me. The good thing is that it is close to school, so I accepted. I start work every day after school, three o'clock."

"And they will pay you? What kind of job will let you resume work at that time? Are you just doing it for the experience?" I wanted to know.

He shifted a shoulder. "Experience and money."

"Why?"

He shrugged and gestured to the children. "We have responsibilities now. You – you've been pulling your weight since they were born. I just want to be able to contribute."

"When I said you needed to be responsible I didn't mean this. I just wanted you to be concerned about them more than you were already, not let your education suffer."

"Trust me, my education will not suffer. If anything, it will be my way of practising what we are taught in class. I think it will even help my education. Besides what do people do after school if not play around? As for reading and assignments, I can do that at night."

"You know if it's because of the money, we are not exactly desperate for it. I and the twins are doing ok with what our parents give us."

"Nah. We can't rely on them forever. It makes me feel guilty. Plus it's fun working. I've only started for two days and I'm really enjoying it." His face lit up as he said that and his lips curved."

"Ehn hen?" I was happy to see him happy, but a growing gloom I could not explain settled in my heart. I tried to mask it by infusing enthusiasm into my voice. "What makes it so much fun?"

"Doing something you will be paid for, there's just this fulfilment in it. I can't explain it but just knowing I'm doing something worthwhile... It makes me happy." His face took on a dreamy expression. "Plus every time I've watched movies and seen people in their offices, sitting on that swivelling chair, I've always dreamt of having that type of life. Well, I don't have my own personal office, but it feels good being in a work environment. It makes me feel grown." His gestures were animated and elaborate. "And the people, oh, the people are so nice and fun to work with."

"Mmm… The girls are very fine abi?"

His eyes looked distant as he smiled and nodded his agreement, then he must have caught my countenance because he quickly became sober.

He sucked his teeth and scratched his head. "I agree they are fine, but I never said they were better than you. Besides I'm not interested in any of them," he stammered, reaching out his hand to touch me, but I slapped it away. I tried not to let the innocent puppy look he was giving affect me.

"It doesn't matter," I said. But it did. It made me feel inadequate. I was angry that it made me want to think of ways to have that look directed at me - the one he had during that brief, unguarded moment when he revealed he appreciated the beauty of other women.

"Look," he pleaded and cupped my chin, his eyes drilling into mine, begging to be believed. His earnestness exaggerated his gestures. "They're just there, just colleagues, nothing more. I have no business with them. You, you are the one I will be with forever. Nothing can separate us. You are the mother of my children after all."

Gently, I removed his hand from my face. I knew his words were meant to reassure, but they did just the opposite. "It all boils down to the children, doesn't it? It isn't about me, or even you for that matter. You would want a choice, but you can't because of them, so you are stuck with me, right? Well, I don't want you wanting me because of them. I don't want you to want me for any other reason except for myself, Obinna. I couldn't bear knowing that. So right now I free you of every attachment. Go ahead, meet new people, make friends, admire as many as you want, and accept love if it finds you. You are free." It took the clenching of all my muscles to hold myself as rigid as I did and pretend it didn't matter when all I wanted to do was desperately force a promise out of him.

"I really do not want to fight." He sounded tired. He looked it too as he rubbed his hand over his face. "Everything I said to you I mean them, ok?"

"Time will tell, Obinna."

Chapter Twelve

Christmas soon came and flew by; as did the next year. I continued with the same routine I had established: dropping the kids off at the day care centre by 7am before leaving for school, attending my lectures, leaving immediately after school to pick the kids and then shuffling studying at night with checking in on sleeping infants gradually growing into toddlers.

At the beginning of my second year, after my first year results were out, I did a calculation of my Cumulative Grade Point Average and celebrated my 4.2 average by fulfilling my dream of experiencing hostel life.

For one whole day I was going to live in the hostel like a real student and do everything students do. I asked Nnenna for help with the twins, who were already sixteen months, and she was pleased to assist. Convincing my parents was the only detail in my well-thought-out plan that kept me thinking for days. Only a reasonable excuse would work with them and I knew I had to make it fool-proof. I came up with many ideas only to discard them after thorough critiquing exposed one loophole or the other, until it was just three days to go and I still had nothing solid.

I planned my stay in school to coincide with the Miss UNILAG beauty pageant. It was the biggest of every social activity held in school. The past one had been what every student unanimously termed 'off the chains'. Students talked about it the entire week and I listened and pined. Now I could live that reality, perhaps even contribute to conversations about the event. Most of all, I would have at least one beautiful memory of my social life in school to save for the future and someday regale my kids with the details.

One of my lecturers would be away on sabbatical for half the semester and needed to rush his lectures through the space of half a semester. To make that possible, he'd been scheduling lectures on some nights and on weekends. I had missed most of the night and weekend lectures, but he fixed a test to hold during one of those night lectures and I couldn't miss that. That was the lie I finally settled on and my parents had no suspicions.

The twins were grown enough to cope without me. I did not need to hurry back after the test, for my safety. It would be better to stay over with Ama in her hostel and return home the following morning, my mother suggested as she helped with plans to ensure I did not miss the test. She was impressed with my result and wanted it to continue that way. Only two people knew my secret, Ama and Nnenna, and I knew they would lose an arm before they thought to expose me.

The night for the pageant came and I was certain I looked like the Nollywood movie depictions of the innocent girl making her first club debut as I walked into the school's main auditorium, gawking at the transformation from the usually drab hall we sometimes used for examinations into a magnificent event space.

Heavy black materials were used as backdrops to cover the walls. Satin and lace materials in various bright colours draped and hung from the ceiling to the walls and down to the floor to give the hall a ceremonial effect. The stage was set too. A welcome message fashioned out of cardboard papers in assorted colours that looked brighter than the rest of the hall was pinned to the backdrop and had stage lights flashing on them. Beside the stage stood the DJ, bobbing his head to the sound blaring out of his sophisticated equipment.

It seemed surreal as I walked down the steps with Ama to look for a suitable seat. Most of the chairs were occupied, the hall was almost full, but we were not too late that we could not find a place to sit. I felt care-free in a way I couldn't remember feeling. Then a wistful feeling surfaced momentarily as I wished my freedom was not short-lived, but I soon pushed that thought away and concentrated on living in the present and savouring every second of it.

Looking around like one who had been starved of social activities and wanting to grab as much of the moment as possible to store up in my memory, I noticed the students all looked different too. Most were not dressed the way they would for lectures. They were dressed for a party; looking alluring, carefree and young. I looked down self-consciously at my yellow snug t-shirt and black jean trousers and concluded that I was lacking. To remedy that, I reached for the rubber band holding my hair up in a ponytail - my favourite hair style - pulled it from my hair onto my wrist, then shook my head, the Darling Yaki weave scattering around my face and shoulders. Feeling wild, I reached for some of the makeup on Ama's lips. She ducked when my finger shot toward her lips, but I held her in place with one hand and, with the index finger of the other, rubbed off some of her red lipstick and applied on my lips. She shook her head at me in amusement.

Feeling considerably confident, I resumed my survey of the students. There were all sorts; the old students standing or sitting and gyrating to the music, the new students sitting shyly, folding into themselves, their body language clearly showing they were new to this experience, yet visibly excited as their eyes darted around, following everything.

My eyes journeyed past a familiar figure at the far end of the hall then flitted back immediately. The object of my distraction was sitting with a female - too close - his head bent toward her as she whispered something into his ears, then he threw his head back to laugh heartily. Despite the heat in the crowded hall, a chill ran through me when he shifted his head and I confirmed it was indeed Obinna. There was something familiar about the woman beside him too, but they were too far off for me to be certain. As I pondered going over there, the voice of the

MC rose over the noise and kept me glued to my seat as he brought the night's event to a start.

By the time the contestants began making their appearances, my excitement had ebbed, to be replaced with defeat. There was no way I could compete with that woman, whoever she was, that I saw with him. I tried to pretend Obinna's actions did not matter and made efforts to concentrate on the models, noting absently that, though pretty, they seemed like more regular, attainable versions of beauty and were nothing like the impossibly perfect models on TV. They sashayed down the catwalk in four different attires; traditional, corporate wear, sportswear and evening gowns, but rather than admire their outfits like I normally would, my head kept turning to look at Obinna and his companion.

I followed the events of the night; the entertainment from popular artistes, jokes from student comedians, yet I also succeeded in following all of Obinna's movements. I wanted desperately to leave that environment, with the happy people in it, for one more befitting of my mood so I could wallow in the self-pity that I could not quite hold off, but looking at Ama, enraptured by the sights on stage and oblivious to my plight, I chose not to spoil her fun. However, mine had been spoiled beyond redemption and I did not think I could ever anticipate or enjoy any social activity again. In the emotion of the moment, I swore silently to dedicate my life to caring for my children and ignore all else, especially trouble which came in the form of good looking boys.

As much as I tried to uphold my resolve to ignore everything else and concentrate on my life and the children's, I lapsed occasionally during that weekend. I caught myself thinking of Obinna a lot and as I did, my emotions oscillated between betrayal and hope. Perhaps if I confronted him he would have an explanation and I would realize I was worried over nothing. I desperately wanted to believe that, yet the saner part of me believed what I saw was as real as it could get and any explanation from him would be a lie. My inner battles must have shown externally because on Sunday night, while I stood in the hallway that led off to the rooms, ironing the clothes to be worn for the entire week, mother sat on the only chair beside the ironing board and looked at me in that way of hers that told me she had been where I was and knew what I was going through.

"Ọgịnị? Did something happen the night you stayed back in school for your test?" She asked, concern deepening the folds at the corners of her eyes and lips. I tamped down the guilt at the reminder of the lie I had told her and Father.

I started to brush off her concern by telling her that nothing had happened, but I needed someone to unload on and she was the available candidate since Ama was in school.

"Yes." I let out a shaky sigh. "After the test, as I was going to Ama's hostel, I saw Obinna with a girl." The lie rolled out easily. "The way they were standing shows that there's something between them."

She shook her head ruefully and was silent for some time. I could see that she was thinking.

"Ada, if you keep watching Obinna and worrying about what he is doing you will always be miserable."

"Mummy, I was not watching him. I was just passing when I saw him."

She waved off my protest. "Whatever the case, you have to try not to let whatever he does or doesn't do affect your state of mind. He might be the father of your children but he is not your husband."

Her words were not making me feel better, which was a rarity, so I tried to end the conversation.

"Ok. I've heard," I said and hoped she would drop the topic. She didn't. Instead she made herself comfortable by settling further into the high stool and resting her back against the wall.

"You see, Ada, when I found out you were pregnant, I immediately started to imagine your future and how far you will be able to go. I was convinced that your situation will change your life and slow you down. I know I urged you on. I did it because that is what a mother should do, but I never thought you will rise easily from your fall. Surprisingly, none of what I anticipated is happening now. Look at you, you haven't lost your pace. If anything you are doing even better than people who have more advantage than you. You need to have more faith in yourself. You amaze me and though your father will not say it to you, he is amazed by you as well. You seem to be the only one who cannot see how extraordinary you are."

"Obinna doesn't see it too."

"There is no one who wouldn't see it. However, how he chooses to react to what he sees in you is out of your control. The more you try to control it, the greater the chances of you undermining yourself."

"So what should I now do? I should just sit and watch him move on to another girl? I should fail my children by letting their father have another family away from them?"

"Will it be better to foist on them a father who doesn't want to stay? There are some things you cannot control, you should leave those things and expend your energy on working on things you can control. I know you feel entitled to him and you may be right, but some things should not be forced, love is one of those things."

I wanted to tell her that I couldn't love anyone else and that I wanted to go to any length to have my love reciprocated, but discussing the issue of love with my mother still made me feel uneasy. It was frustrating being unable to explain how I felt to her, so I tried to communicate my feelings in the only way I could and hoped she would read beyond the inadequacy of my words.

"Mummy, I don't know. I just don't know. I am tired." I reached for the switch and flicked it off then leaned heavily on the ironing board. I felt too weak to stand on my own but worse than that, I felt miserable. I saw no reason to hide it. "I am so sad."

"I can't ask you not to be sad, Ada, because I know the feeling will not go away just because I say so. All I can ask you to do is to try and concentrate on other things aside from Obinna and a future with him."

She stood and picked some hangers from the basket beside the board and took her time hanging the ironed clothes arranged on one end of the ironing board. I joined her.

"I never knew I would be saying this to you because it has always been my hope that you will find a nice man, settle down with him and start a family, but there are so many things more important in life than marriage. Self-actualization is one of those things."

Gently, she placed one hanged dress on the chair she vacated, then picked another from the ironing board and started to hang it.

"Your situation is no longer the same as that of most girls. For you, with children, it will be harder to get a husband." I tried to interrupt but she held up a hand. "I know you feel that is the more reason why you should hold on to Obinna, but you cannot hold people like you do things. The best thing for you to do now is to find a way to gain that advantage you have lost, and the way you can achieve that is by working on improving yourself so that you are too good to be ignored. Success attracts friends. Once you are successful everyone will want to associate with you, then you can have your pick of the best men and if you get a husband out of it, fine, if you don't your life is far from over. Again, I can't believe I am saying this, but your worth is not defined by having a man in your life and your life can be perfectly fulfilling with or without a man. So from what I see now, you have two choices." She counted off the choices on her fingers. "To worry over a boy and disgrace yourself by fighting for his attention or to develop yourself and have people fighting to have your attention. You are your mother's child Ada. Choose wisely."

By Monday afternoon I had convinced myself it would be best to follow mother's advice, but to do so I needed to have some sort of closure in order to be able to lay my feelings for Obinna to rest. For that reason, I decided to meet him after school.

I rehearsed my speech on the way to his faculty building and as I got close I was fairly confident that I had everything covered. I later realized that a part of me also hoped that after my speech he would beg to remain in my life.

I got to the front of his class and the confidence I had built up fled. There he stood, an intense expression on his face, as he listened to a girl. I could only see her back but I knew she was the one he had been with three nights ago at the main auditorium.

My well prepared speech vanished from my memory and I stood immobile as I wondered what to do next. He had not seen me. I could leave quietly and forget about getting the closure I sought. I wondered if it would be cowardly, then decided I was past caring. I almost turned, but curiosity kept me rooted to the spot. I had to know who she was at least. While I was still contemplating how to approach the situation, Obinna looked up, saw me and looked startled.

I started toward them, quickly improvising. As I got close, the girl, obviously alerted by the look on Obinna's face, turned, and her eyes widened in recognition. I was surprised too to see Abike but I had a sudden idea. Schooling my features to hide my surprise, I looked at her with curiosity and smiled.

"Ahn ahn. Ada, what are you doing here?" she asked.

I feigned a look of sincere apology. "Sorry I'm not Ada. I'm Ama."

From the corner of my eye I noticed Obinna's brows shoot up to his forehead. Most people could not tell us apart but Obinna could.

"Ama? And I've been calling you Ada all this while."

"Ada is my sister."

"Oh wait…You mean Ada has a twin? I didn't know," she said, looking shocked. Her reaction was no different from what I get all the time from people who realize much later that I have an identical twin.

I smiled sweetly. "Are you Ada's friend?"

"Well, not really. God, I can't believe it. There's almost no difference." She shook her head in disbelief. "I am Abike, her dean's secretary."

"Nice to meet you, Abike." I offered my hand for a handshake and she took it, still looking at me with her mouth hanging open. "So you are a staff member? You look like a student."

"I'm a staff member and a student; a part-time student." She did look like a student; young and fresh and, though it was painful to admit it, very beautiful. I had no idea she was schooling and my surprise this time was genuine.

"Wow. That's impressive. It must be hard, schooling and working."

"Well, it's not easy o, which is why I am impressed with Obinna who is working and schooling full time. At least mine is just part time." She stopped and frowned. "You know each other?"

I nodded. "He is a family friend."

Obinna who had been silently following our conversation spoke then. "Em, Ada, sorry Ama, can we talk in my class?"

"Ehen! You see? Even someone who is your family friend can't tell you two apart. You are so identical. I can't wait to tell Ada I saw her twin."

Obinna started to lead me into his class after Abike left, but I shrugged off his hand and pinned him with an accusing stare.

He passed a hand over his head and planted his feet apart in front of me like he was expecting a fight. "She is just a junior colleague, Ada, and why did you have to pretend to be Ama?"

I let out a short bitter laugh, ignoring his question. "A junior colleague? She isn't even a regular student."

"I know, but she sometimes attends lectures with regular students and she comes to me for help with courses she has problems with, that's how I got to know her. There's nothing between us. We are never together after school hours."

"Really? You have become good at lying Obinna. I saw both of you together on the night of Miss Unilag." I enjoyed seeing him look flustered at my revelation. I knew I was acting childish, but I did not want to stop.

"God. That was the only time." He raised both hands then let them fall to his sides and exhaled audibly.

My lips curved but there was no humour in it. I was tired of trying, tired of hoping and most of all tired of setting myself up to be hurt. I had come for closure and none could be better than the one I walked in on. As always, mother was right; some things cannot be controlled. So, standing there before the only boy I had ever wanted, my heart broken, I made my choice. "Have a nice life Obinna."

It wasn't pain I felt as I side stepped to avoid his grasp and made my exit from his faculty block. It was calmness, a total lack of feeling that numbed my senses and I was both grateful for, and afraid of it.

Chapter Thirteen

I did fine, better than I expected.

Obinna and I saw often and we kept it civil, but I had no more expectations of him. Following mother's advice to make myself better, I put away the need to have a social life like other students and threw myself into studying every free time I had. I also stayed away from the dean's office.

One afternoon, halfway into our first semester exams, I submitted my ACC 201 exam paper and stepped out of the class with the aim of getting something to eat before the next paper. I had such a strong craving for the *moin-moin* sold by Aunty Patience behind the Humanities Faculty that I could almost taste it. As I stood, wondering whether to satisfy my craving and go all the way to Humanities block or make do with what was available close to my faculty block, someone tickled my waist and I turned back to face Abike.

The resentment came swiftly and it obviously registered on my face because I saw her eyes shift in confusion. With conscious effort, I reminded myself to stay calm and continue with the pretence. I smiled and waited for her to keep moving.

"It's you I came here to look for," she said brightly and slapped my shoulder playfully. I didn't bother to reply, my raised brows did the questioning.

"Yes now. I haven't seen you in a long time. You. You ehn." She wagged her finger in front of my face. "You are so secretive. How come you don't tell people that you have a twin?"

"Because I don't want you people to come and carry us and throw in the evil forest."

She laughed and hit my shoulder again. "You ehn. You are just funny. Anyway, I saw your twin in Architecture block with Obinna."

"Oh," I said simply and waited for her to leave.

"Ehen!" As if remembering suddenly, she slapped her palms together then pushed my shoulder again but with more force this time. "Why didn't you tell me you know Obinna?"

Moving away from the door to free the entrance for those exiting my class, I made a huge show of looking at my watch, hoping she'd take the cue. "So I'm supposed to write the names of everyone I know and come and submit to you?"

Unperturbed, she pushed my question aside with a hand gesture. "Anyway, who is he to you?"

Exasperated now, I wanted to scream at her and walk away, I almost did, then I remembered the warning that it isn't wise to get on her bad side. She might have become quite friendly, even respectful, toward me but she was still the same person.

"Family friend."

"Ehn hen? Tell me the truth." She leaned closer and whispered conspiratorially. "Is he dating your sister?"

"Why will you think that?" I desperately needed an escape, but could not think of one, so I hoped for Kosi to quickly finish writing her exam and be the excuse I needed to leave.

"The way I saw them... You know I can read people well. Like the first time you came into my office, I just knew you were not just any student. When I saw your sister with Obinna, the look between them... It was as if they are dating, but were quarrelling. Is she his girlfriend?"

"No, they are not dating. See, Abike, I'm hungry. I want to go and eat before my next paper."

"Ehn, no problem. Let's go together."

As we walked down the corridor, my course mates gave us curious stares, no doubt wondering what Professor Okoro's formidable secretary was doing with me. I walked slightly slower to be a step behind her but she slowed her pace to match mine. I worried being with her would discredit me in the sight of my colleagues and make them careful around me, especially since they always openly criticised her in class.

"Ada, I really like that Obinna guy. He is so fine. Can you connect me?" Her request hit me like a blow and I felt dizzy. The detachment I had worked to achieve vanished faster than it took me to build and possessiveness took over. Even before I spoke, I knew it was a bad idea. I tried to swallow my words but they tumbled out.

"I cannot. He's my children's father."

Her face was a study in shock, her eyes almost bulged out of its sockets and her jaw slacked. Then she smiled. "Stop lying joor."

"For real, he is." Already at the shop closest to my faculty building, I ordered a bottle of Sprite and a sausage roll and relished the silence following my revelation. Varying expressions crossed her face, showing she was doing serious thinking. I was thinking too, whether I must offer to buy her something to eat or not.

"Are you hungry?" I hoped she would not accept. She declined and held my arm, pulling me out of the crowded shop to a corner where it was just the two of us.

"I thought you told me you have a husband."

"Did I tell you that or you assumed?"

"Ehn, it doesn't matter. The thing is you and Obinna are not married so…" She shrugged and left the sentence open for me to interpret however I chose.

The implication of her words filled me with dread and I began to imagine a future where her life was linked to mine forever. The possibility of her winning Obinna's love and bearing children who share the same father as my children had me panicking. With commendable effort, I suppressed the panic with the reasoning that he would never want to marry a woman older than him. Most importantly, Aunty Oyedinma, his mother, was as traditional as she was proper and would lose her sanity before she allowed her only child to marry a woman from another tribe. That reassured me a little.

"No, we are not married, but know one thing, Abike, Obinna will never marry you. Take it from me. You can try, you don't need my help to get him, but try all you want, with or without assistance from me, you will never have him."

Unable to control it, I gave her a baleful look. I no longer feared her. If anything I saw her as one of us, a student, and felt there was no reason to feel threatened by her. In return, her lips curved with a sinister smile that would have had any student trembling and she snapped threatening fingers at me before turning her back to me.

Chapter Fourteen

When I was in primary school I looked forward to the last Saturday of the month, which was environmental sanitation day. On this day, we were allowed to run around, both within and outside the compound, while the adults cleaned up. The sun was always out on these Saturdays. I do not remember anytime when it rained on sanitation day, and the best part was always after the inside cleaning was done and they started with the outside.

I loved dragging a rake across the floor, doing what I thought was a fine job of gathering dirt together, while I listened to my parents and other adults have interesting grown-up conversations and tell jokes. Adult jokes have always held a fascination for me, even the ones I did not understand. Every time, after listening to them, I would ask my mother the meaning of something that had made them smile which I did not understand and she would silence me by scolding that it was rude to listen to adults' conversation. But that never stopped me from listening, I only stopped asking. It was always a pleasure to watch them dissolve into laughter and this would have me doubled over with laughter too when mother was not present to rebuke me with a threatening look from those eyes that spoke more than words could. When she was present, I just smiled and bent my head to hide it.

When I was old enough and was expected to actively take part in sanitation, the moment it stopped being a game and turned to real work,

I stopped enjoying it and did everything I could to avoid it; from claiming I had cramps to locking myself up in the toilet with the excuse that I was stooling, until I ran out of believable excuses.

The last Saturday in July was one of those mornings when I could not find any excuse to avoid clean-up. The heat from the sun was still mild as I swept together the weeds I had spent the better part of thirty minutes uprooting and threw them into the large dustbin beside the gate leading in and out of our compound. My sisters, every one of them, including Ama who was home due to the ASUU strike, were positioned at different spots in the compound, sweeping or raking. Situations had changed and we the kids now did the cleaning. My mother was inside, perhaps still sleeping, and my dad was in front of his car tinkering with the engine. The children were climbing around him, laughing and causing him to laugh. Their joy was infectious and made me wish I could be that little again, my only worry being school and homework.

Emeka and Chuka stood on the bench my father placed in front of the car so they could reach into the engine. He hit around with a spanner then laughed when Chuka imitated him. He opened the radiator and allowed Emeka pour water into it. Chika started to climb onto the bench but could not on her own so she wobbled to her granddaddy and pulled on his legs to be lifted up. He bent and offered her a winsome smile then patted her cheek with the heel of his palm to keep the dirt on his hand from staining her skin. Chika smiled and that made me smile too.

"Up. Up," she said, stretching on tiptoe, arms raised towards my father.

My father shook a finger at her. "This..." he pointed to the car engine. "Not for you."

Chika started to whimper and rock in protest. To pacify her, he nudged her to the car then opened the driver's door for her, but she screamed in frustration and ran back to the bonnet stretching her hand towards Emeka and Chuka. As Chuka reached down to help her up, I caught the look my father sent my way and I hurried to get her out.

"Leave her alone!" Nnenna straightened from the gutter she was sweeping to glare at my father and me. We both gave her a look that questioned her sanity and I continued dragging a protesting Chika.

"Why can't she be there if she wants to?"

"Do you want her to injure herself? If she does will you pay for her treatment?"

"Are Emeka and Chuka immune to injury? Yet you let them stay. Why can't she stay too since she wants to?"

We both looked at her again in disbelief. I feared my father would rebuke her. His face clouded over for a moment, making me certain he would, and she must have noticed it too because fear crept into her daring eyes. Instead, he shook his head and turned to the car while I shook mine and, smiling ruefully, carried Chika up and into the house. Nnenna threw her broom down with such force and stomped after me into the house all the while grumbling loudly so my father could hear.

I was silent when Nnenna stormed into the room, prancing around and huffing, like a volcano bubbling and about to spill. I was silent when her eyes glinted and her restless hands lifted clothes from the bed and threw them aside because I knew she wanted me to talk. I knew that all she needed was just the most minimal prompt from me to have all that heat spilling. From experience, I was certain someone was going to get scalded when it did, so I busied myself rocking an inconsolable Chika. When she wouldn't stop crying, I was tempted to scold but put a lid on my temper. I had two rebellious females on my hands and I was not going to give them a reason to make me the recipient of their outburst.

"I guess I better accept that Emeka is more important than the rest of us in this house." Nnenna hissed and threw her weight on the bed she had cleared. The springs whined in protest.

"Are you envious of your own brother? He's just a baby!"

"I'm not envious of him. I just detest the way things are. And I detest that you all make it seem okay and make me feel like a deviant for wanting things to be different. I have always wanted different, but no one will let me have it. Now they are giving it all to Emeka without caring if he wants it or not. It's just unfair."

"Nnenna, I hate to be one of those to make you feel like a deviant for wanting what you want but what have we ever wanted in this house that was denied us?"

"Everything! Everything that ever *really* mattered to me. How many times did I beg daddy to teach me to drive or about cars and he refused? But he lets Emeka and Chuka play around with him under the car. Every night we stay in darkness until daddy comes back to put on the generator by himself just because he will not show me how to do it, even though I've begged him. The only time we are allowed near the generator is when it's time to clean it. Should I go on? And when I ask why I can't do it he'll say, 'Ọ n'imarọ n'ibu nwanyi?' I'm a girl, and so what? God! I'm tired of hearing that. Mummy's own is even worse. If you sit like this, or laugh like that, or even run around in the house she will remind you that you are a girl."

"Well, it's common manners to behave properly," I pointed out.

"Common manners for girls alone? Because I know she doesn't mind when a boy does all those things. I am tired. I really am. These restrictions annoy me in a way nobody understands. I just want to be everything I want to be and do everything I want to do without someone reminding me that I am a girl and should not."

"I'm afraid I don't understand you Nnenna. Give it time, maybe this is just a phase that will pass."

"No, it is not. I will always feel this way. I will always feel angry each time you carry Chika with you into the kitchen and drive Chuka away when he comes in. You are no different, you see? You are doing the same thing with your children."

"Well because I see it as the right way."

"Is it? Well, I hate to cook! But who has ever asked me? I must cook every Tuesday and Friday when it's my turn."

"But Nnenna you love to cook. Will you deny that now just to win an argument?" I was perplexed.

"No. I hate it. And I hate sweeping, but I must do them all, else they will chase me from my husband's house. Isn't that what mummy always says? Yet does anyone chase a husband from the house when he loses his job and can't perform his role of providing for the family, since we have decided to assign roles to people whether they want it or not?"

I wanted to tell her that there were roles which men had and could not escape from too; to draw her attention to the privileges women enjoy. A woman could decide she did not want to have a paying job, she could stay at home without anyone judging her, whereas, a man did not have the choice to be a stay-at-home dad. Society would frown at his choice and call him lazy. It was on the tip of my tongue to bring that up and score a point in the argument, but knowing Nnenna, I was sure that would only increase her determination to prove her point so I let it slide, choosing instead to explain to her why roles were necessary.

"It's not just about assigning roles, Nnenna. This is about responsibility. If there were no set roles, no one will be held accountable for anything and that's a recipe for disaster. That's what differentiates children from adults; children do what they like to do, but adults do what they have to do, whether they like it or not. That's why the roles are there. Just get used to it."

I turned to leave the room and hopefully end the discussion, but she pulled me back by my arm.

"Are you not tired of people telling you what you should do or shouldn't do?" Standing at almost the same height with me, her eyes drilled into mine, searching for answers there, as though the words out of my lips could not be trusted.

"Well, I am not doing anything I don't want to do."

"Maybe that's because you have become so used to the life you've been leading that you see what people expect of you as what you really want for yourself. OK look at it like this, what if you never had any idea of what is expected of a woman or a man? What if you never knew what was expected from you and you could do or be just anything at all, what would you be or do differently?"

"Well..." I considered this for a while then shrugged. "Nothing. I'll still be who I am, doing what I am doing."

She groaned in frustration and started to walk out. My next words stopped her.

"Well, maybe I will want to be able to live in the hostel within campus or just outside of campus, instead of going to school from home because I'm a mother."

She clapped her palms together in excitement. "You see? That's exactly what I'm talking about. Obinna can do that, though he's in the same boat as you, yet his life hasn't been altered greatly because of it, like yours has. He can still do every single thing he was doing before he became a father, but not you. You can't. Why? You know why."

I was upset that I was already warming up to her opinion. It made me a bad mother to resent doing the needful by my kids, so I fought the thought.

"Actually I don't mind doing all that. I like my life the way it is now. What is so special about experiencing hostel life anyway?" I lied, pretending it didn't bother me to never have that experience I imagined having all through secondary school.

"You are lying and you know it."

"A good mother sacrifices."

"So should a good father."

"He works. For us. Do you think it's easy closing from school every day and going straight to work?"

"Because he wants to. Because he loves the job. You want to live in school and live a free life, but you can't. He can."

"Well, if not me, who else?"

"Why not him?" She asked and I thought she was crazy to even consider that. My expression must have communicated my thought because she held up a hand and warned. "Don't look at me like I'm crazy. It's true. Why not him?" When I tried to argue she stopped me with a raised palm. "It all just brings us back to where we started – you don't have the choice to do whatever you want. A woman must suffer to be considered a virtuous woman and a good mother, whether she likes it or not. Even if she works, she is required to come back home to the house chores and all the other things involved in running a home. And a man… well, he can conquer the world and do anything he wants. Tell me that is fair and I'll tell you you don't know what fair means."

"Well, that's the way things are. I doubt if anything can be done to change that."

She looked sad as she considered, then as if waking from a trance, she blinked and shook her head. "There's nothing that is permanent, Ada. That's my only hope. Anything can change given time. I refuse to accept this way as the only way."

Ama's voice calling from the parlour to inform me that Kingsley was looking for me ended my discussion with Nnenna and quickened my pulse.

The young man I met in the parlour had little resemblance to the Kingsley I knew. He was darker, or maybe it was the dark beard covering most of his chin and upper lip that made him look so. Though sitting, his legs stretched out in front of him, extending beneath the centre table. When his eyes met mine and he stood to hug me, my observation was confirmed, he was taller and not just by a few inches. His hair cut had changed also and he now let his hair grow a bit higher with the edges carved neatly. He had lost his timidity and looked self-assured.

"You look like a celeb." I did not think before I said that one, but I made sure not to voice my other thought, which is that he smelled exotic. His scent was inviting without being intrusive.

"That's not true. I haven't changed much." He spread out his arms as proof, but all my brain registered was the strong forearms exposed by the rolled up sleeve, the veins twisting down them looked like branches. "You are the one who has changed."

"Don't lie, no one has told me that."

"You have changed. You look finer." He insisted. His words made me feel confident and special. I wanted to hear it often and in the same sincere tone he used.

"You are just saying it to keep conversation going. You know it." I knew I was fishing for compliment but I continued without shame.

"No, I am not. Except my eyes now fail me, and if there's any part of my anatomy that is in perfect condition it will be my eyes. And my heart." he added and gave me a meaningful look. "And they both like what they see in you."

Delighted, I lowered myself to the chair closest to him and he sat too. "I see you went to UNICAL to master the art of sweet talking, abi?"

He laughed and looked at me. I decided that he had mastered the art of staring as well. His gaze was captivating in such a way that I could not avert mine. "I saw your son outside. He's so grown now. He has your nose and your smile," he pointed to my face. "What of his sister?"

"She's inside with Nnenna."

"Nnenna, firebrand!"

"As in! She hasn't changed o." I left him to get refreshment and from the kitchen raised my voice so he could hear me. "So the strike finally caught up with your school, ehn?"

"We've been on strike for the past three months o. I stayed back, hoping it will end soon. There were rumours in the South-South that the strike will not last, but with the way things are going Christmas will come and meet us still on strike."

"Ha. I hope not o. I'm tired of staying at home." I joined him in the parlour, pulling a side stool close to him. On it, I placed the tray loaded with a bottle of malt and the soft *chin chin* I made the night before for Chika who could never have enough. "I can't wait to finish school. By now we should have started third year."

"Everybody is already considering an alternative for school. Guys are thinking of which business to start and many girls are now married."

"My dear, you didn't lie. Many of my course mates have married during this strike. If care is not taken when the strike ends some may not return to school."

He opened the bottle and, throwing back his head, swallowed most of its content in one gulp. I stared in fascination at his Adam's apple as it bobbed up and down. He caught me staring and flashed a charming grin.

"So, are you planning to toe that line and get married this strike too?"

I humphed. "No."

"Why? Obinna is not ready? His parents have money, they can sponsor him."

"Obinna and I are not together anymore."

"Oh." He grabbed a handful of chin chin and threw them into his mouth, one at a time. I was relieved that he did not pursue the topic. He did not stay for long and when he was about to leave he gave N200 each to Emeka, Chika and Chuka.

"There's this new eatery at Adetola I hear makes the best Shawarma in Aguda. Will you like to try it out tomorrow?" Hands in the pockets of his casual cargo shorts, Kingsley moved slowly beside me as I saw him off.

I had never eaten Shawarma and badly wanted to try it. I had not been out socially in a while too, yet I hesitated, though I could not understand why. He sensed my hesitation as well and that caused him to sigh deeply.

"Ada, you've been running from me since SS1. When will you stop?"

"I am just trying to make the right decisions, not running. Things are complicated for me since I have children. I can't just make decisions lightly anymore because they will affect not just me, but the children and Obinna."

He muttered beneath his breath and slammed a fist against his thigh. Frustration was evident on his features. "Why do you have to mention Obinna? You haven't gotten over him. I can feel it. You even have to consider him when you are making decisions."

"Yes, because he is my children's father and what affects us will invariably affect him. That's all. There's nothing more between us."

"Your children are the reason you can't forget Obinna. They are the reason you won't give me a chance. Sometimes I wish you never had kids."

His words stopped me in my tracks and I inhaled sharply as though I'd been punched in the stomach. I regretted getting pregnant early without being married. I regretted the life I couldn't live because I was a mother, but ever since I put to bed, not once did I regret the presence of my children in my life or wish I could have a life without them. Hearing someone voice the wish that they never existed tugged at something vicious in me. I wanted to jump on him and rip through him until he was a mass of flesh, blood, and bones plastered on the tarred road; instead, I took deep breaths to pull myself together.

Oblivious to the effect his words had on me, he started to talk, looked at me, then seeing the look on my face, he gasped.

"Hey. God. Ada, I didn't mean it that way. I just… Please, I'm sorry." He held his hands out toward me in sincere apology. "You know I like your children."

The fight went out of me the way it came - suddenly.

"It's OK. As for tomorrow, I won't be able to meet with you." I quickly dismissed him even as he protested and went home to gather Chika and Chuka in a tight embrace that had Nnenna raising her brows at me.

Chapter Fifteen

The strike continued for two more months.

When we finally resumed in October there was a rush to finish second semester before the year ended in order to meet up with the next academic calendar and admit new students. We were already writing second semester exams even before most of our first semester results were out. There was no time to do anything else except study and the pregnant students in our midst, of which there were many, took the worst hit.

By January, I was already in third year. On the first day of school, before going into my new class, I stopped at the department's notice board to check the results pasted that morning. I was elated with my grades until I got to ECO 201 and found that I had no result in the course.

Too troubled to sit through lectures because of the issue with my result, I abandoned my first lecture to seek out Abike. I was prepared for animosity, so her smile took me by surprise.

"Hey, Ada. Happy new year."

"Same to you," I returned her greeting.

"Longest time. Are you now avoiding me? How are you and your children, and Obinna too?" She wriggled her brow and smiled mischievously as she said his name, causing me to laugh.

"We are fine." I did not sit when the pleasantries were out of the way.

"Abike, my result is missing in Professor. Okoro's course."

"Ahn ahn. How come?"

"I don't know o. What am I supposed to do now?"

She took me through the process; I was to write a letter to the Exams and Records department informing them of my missing result, then submit the typed letter to be signed by the lecturer who taught that course. Afterwards, the lecturer would check the exam attendance sheet to confirm I took the exam, then sign and send the letter to the Exams and Records department to have them search through the exam sheets for mine. If found, my script would be forwarded to the lecturer to mark and record my score.

"And how long will it take?" It sounded like a complicated process.

"It depends." She shrugged. "It could be one week, it could be months, sometimes it will not even be found until the next set are writing the exam and you'll have to carry it over."

I was distraught and spent the next hours seeking out students who have had missing results in the past. I collected samples of their application letter to use as a template for mine, had the letter typed when I was done drafting, and returned to Abike with it that same day.

"So when will this get to Professor Okoro's desk?" I asked when she slid the letter into a drawer rather than stand to take it into the dean's office as I expected.

"Before close of work today. Don't worry, you'll find your result, you hear? Come back when school closes to check if he has signed it so that you can follow it up with the people at Exams and Records."

After my lectures, for the third time that day, I returned to meet with Abike who remained kind and helpful.

"Has he signed?"

"No. He left for senate meeting. But it's on his desk now. See, why not give him time and come by 3 pm tomorrow. It must be ready then. I'm sure you're in a hurry to go and pick your children now. Is their school near here?"

"No o. It's at Aguda where I live. One Greenhill Nursery and Primary school like that."

"Are they in nursery or primary?"

"They are still in kindergarten." I gestured with my hand toward the ground to show how small they still are.

"Ah, that means you still have a long way to go with paying school fees and everything. O ga o." She lifted her right arm above her head, fist clenched, and shook it in the way one would when hailing a powerful person. She quickly added, "See me that I'm even talking. I've not even started giving birth. My own journey is still far."

As I was about to leave, she called me back and suggested an easier alternative. The staff at the Exams and Records department were usually overwhelmed at this time and may be slow in searching for my result, she said. She offered to have a junior staff from our faculty assist the E&R staff to search for my exam paper. All I had to do, according to her, was to write a note giving the junior staff my permission to act on my behalf. My signature and the dean's signature would be on the note. Abike gave me a sheet of paper and dictated what I should write.

"Kindly grant him full access to act on my behalf," she said and I wrote and signed.

Chapter Sixteen

Our misfortunes, even the minor ones, usually seem extremely nightmarish until a worse calamity befalls us making the former seem benign in comparison.

My aspiration was being threatened and it bothered me too much as I sat waiting for Professor Okoro the next day. It was 4 P.M. and I decided I would leave if he did not return within the next ten minutes. I had tried leaving a couple of times, but Abike kept assuring me he would be back soon, so I called mother and asked her to help me pick the twins from day care.

Things were looking good. My second-year average, when calculated without the missing result, was at 4.6 CGPA. There was a chance I could exceed my expectations and graduate with a first class after all. I could already imagine the glory of it and the more I thought about it, the greater my distress at the missing result which could jeopardize that dream. Determined to see the search of my result through to the end, I continued to wait.

Just as soon as I decided that Professor Okoro probably had no plans of returning and going home was the sensible thing to do, my phone rang. It was noisy in the background, a chatter of voices talking animatedly, and I had to strain to make out mother's words.

"Ada, did you tell Obinna to pick Chuka them after you called me?"

"Obinna? No o. Someone that must be at work now."

She paused but her breathing was heavy through the phone and that pricked my senses.

"Mummy, what is it?"

"Nothing. Just start coming to their school now."

"Why?" Dread clutched my heart and squeezed till I was panting.

She didn't answer immediately. When she did, she sounded calm and slightly irritated and that reassured me. "They won't let me pick them. They said you informed them this morning that only their father should be allowed to pick them."

"What nonsense. Give Aunty Shade the phone," I ordered, waiting for her to pass the phone to the childminder responsible for my kids, but she declined.

"See, Ada, no need. Just start coming fast. She has refused to release them until she sees you. I don't know why she's doing as if she does not know me again."

Once I entered the school premises, I sensed something was amiss. It was past five, yet the school was still filled with parents and teachers who stood in clusters shaking their heads and cupping their chins. When their eyes met mine, it seemed to me that they were looking at me with pity. I hurried along, crossing the assembly ground to the wing that has the kindergarten classes.

Mother came out carrying Emeka to hug me and led me into the class. My heart beat increased with each step and so did the feeling of doom.

Two uniformed police officers were in the class with a teary Aunty Shade. The class was otherwise empty.

"Where are my children?" I looked from my children's minder to my mother and my mother's eyes welled up.

"They said a man came, claiming that you sent him to pick them."

My feet gave way beneath me and I fell to be caught by mother before I hit the ground. I felt dizzy and every object in sight seemed to be swimming. I could hear the voice of the policewoman but it seemed to be coming from a distance and her words wouldn't register. Then mother shook me vigorously and everything came into focus at once. Aunty

Shade was jumping with her hands on her head and at the same time screaming in her local dialect. Emeka looked alarmed, then suddenly let out a piercing cry. Mother tried to console him while holding on to me as the female police officer squatted beside me and looked at me with stern eyes.

I answered her questions, balked at the insinuations and denied her accusations that I might have planned it to extort money from Obinna's influential parents and that my grief didn't seem genuine. I was too occupied with imagining where the twins were to be as offended by her as I should have been. Rocking back and forth, my mind darted to events of the past and people who might want to harm my children. I could not think of anyone to blame so I turned it inwards, blaming myself instead.

My last moment with them was spent worrying about my missing result so that I did not give them the attention I would have, had I known they would be gone soon. It was also following up with the result that kept me from picking them early, thereby leaving them vulnerable to a predator. At that point, the missing result seemed so inconsequential. There was a second chance to rewrite that exam but I would never have another chance to birth the exact same babies stolen from me. My heart broke some more at the thought and I sobbed until it was impossible to answer any more questions.

When the questioning was over and it was obvious that waiting in school would no longer yield any result, mother took me home against the wishes of the officers who wanted me to follow them to the station to make a statement. Emeka had to be fed and I needed to calm down. She promised I would report to the station later that day.

When tragedy knocks on your door, everyone becomes an expert and develops an opinion on what you've been doing wrong.

They tell you what is wrong with your system of doing things, even though they had hitherto been fine with it. Then they proceed to offer suggestions of what you should have done differently - suggestions they would never have considered, but which they do now having learnt from your mistake. Things are taken for granted all the time, but the one whose mistake cost something great and ends in tragedy becomes the lesson. Ways of life that were the norm and the general practice become condemned, even by all those who never had a problem with them. Everyone becomes an adviser and the victim is burdened with pity at best and criticisms at worst.

I, also, saturated with grief, began to consider alternate choices I could have made to avert this tragedy. Perhaps if I had chosen a different school with tighter security, if I had skipped every lecture that ended later than my kids' closing time and gone to pick them earlier... Choices no one would have considered except they had a premonition of what was to come, or with the wisdom of hindsight, presented themselves and made me feel like a careless mother.

I was inconsolable. It was an effort to breathe as I listened to advice from sympathisers that did nothing to help my sanity.

"You should have specifically instructed their teacher not to let anyone pick them, even if it is your mother," a neighbour whose grandchildren go to the same school as my children said.

I didn't bother to explain that a number of people, my mother and sisters included, pitched in to help pick them up when I could not make it early.

"The mistake you made was not giving the teacher a picture of everyone allowed access to the kids. Every mother should know that," a young mother said.

No mother in my children's school did that and no one scolded them for not doing so. My mother, God bless her, came to my rescue.

"Does your child's teacher have pictures of every member of your family?"

"Erm... No ... But it's not... she knows I am the only one allowed to pick them," she stammered, thrown off by mother's question. Then regaining her composure, she continued more assuredly. "She will never allow anyone, not even my husband, to go near them without calling me first to confirm. Anyway, the mistake has been made. Next time, just be more careful."

Hearing her say 'next time' made it sound as though it was already too late this time to right things. I pleaded with God to help me find them and promised there would not be a next time because I would never let them out of my sight again.

The whispers from the men squeezed my heart even more.

Mothers need to learn to be more careful with their children.

What nonsense schooling was she doing? Couldn't she leave school until the children were grown? Now see what has happened. Will all her education help to bring her children home?

These small girls that don't even know how to take care of themselves will go and be having children.

I knew the true meaning of a broken heart and nothing I felt after separating from Obinna, when I thought I was heartbroken, came close. I never wanted to hear anyone insult the meaning of that word by using it with regards to the end of a relationship. Only death or the loss of a loved one could shred the heart so. Food became repulsive, the idea of sleeping made me feel guilty, and reality and nightmare merged. My life as I knew it stood still while a horror movie, unending, stretched out in its place.

Chapter Seventeen

The reception area of the Soloki police station in Aguda looked depressing. Wooden backed chairs with torn cushions revealing the foam and spring beneath rested against the dark grey wall. There was a high reception desk separating the visitors in the sitting area from the two police officers sitting on high stools behind the desk. The football match showing on the TV screen hanging on the wall had the officers' attention and we had to greet a third time before the female officer acknowledged our greeting with a raised hand and immediately turned back to the game. The male officer's eyes never shifted from the screen.

The single light bulb suspended from the ceiling gave off a dim light that barely lit the top of the reception desk. The rest of the room was cast in shadows. Candlelight would have worked better at lighting the room. Even with the light from the television supplementing, the room was still inadequately lit. There were four visitors - three men and a woman - seated around on the chairs, wearing the expectant look of people waiting. Their faces looked hollow and their eyes appeared haunted, all of them. I hoped it was the dim lighting giving them that effect.

When no one said anything to us, mother spoke up. "We were told to come and make a statement. And I want to know what progress you --"

The male officer slapped his hand down impatiently against the table, effectively hushing mother. "Wait, somebody will attend to you."

We waited, all of us standing, holding onto each other to draw strength. I felt sorry for Obinna who, having no one to lean on, stood aside looking forlorn. Moving slightly away from mother's embrace, I held out a hand to him. Our eyes met; in his were unshed tears and tension. I wanted to hug him tight but because of the presence of my parents, I settled for a hand squeeze.

Heavy approaching footsteps caused me to look up and I saw, first, a large stomach preceding a tall, huge man into the room. His black uniform stretched against his beer gut and the buttons running down the middle threatened to rip. Breathing must have been hard for him judging by the wheezing sound made when he spoke.

"Yes?" he asked around a mouthful of food.

"My children were taken from Greenhill School today by someone we don't know."

"Oh, so na you be the mama wey leave im pikin dem make another person go carry?"

Mother and father gaped in shock at his insensitivity. Father charged forward and raised a finger to the policeman but the hand came down when mother squeezed his shoulder and whispered something to him.

"Don't talk to her like that," Obinna warned. He was shaking now just as he had been when he rushed into our parlour after work demanding to know what the call put through to him meant. When the visitors at my house dished subtle criticisms, he shook in anger. As we stood in the station, I realized the shaking had to do with more than just anger. For all his brave front, the fear beneath was visible to me.

"Who you be?" the police officer jerked his head in Obinna's direction.

"I'm the father."

"Na you born am?" He pointed his chin at me, looking incredulous. He seemed to be doing a lot of pointing with his head and I guessed it had to do with the tightness of his shirt not permitting movement.

"Not her. I'm the children's father."

He shook his head and turned down the corners of his lips in disdain muttering something we couldn't hear.

"Una don receive any call from the pesin wey carry your pikin dem?"

Waiting to hear our phones ring had been as frightening as finding out the children had been taken. After hours of waiting, I began to wonder if a call would ever come in. The twins were only two years and did not know any of our phone numbers. If anyone called, claiming to be with the children, one thing would be clear at least, that the kidnapper knew us well enough to have our phone numbers. But no call had come through and we told the officer that.

"Where are officers Kabiru and Ngozi? They were the ones we met at the school and I promised them I will bring my daughter to the station."

"Na officer Kabiru dem you want abi na the children you want?" he retorted.

Mother's answer was to turn her mouth downwards. Still chewing, he opened a book on the reception desk and turned it to me.

"Take." He handed me a pen. "Write wetin happen."

Confused, I looked from the book to him. It was my first time ever in a police station. I had never written a statement and did not understand what was expected.

"I don't know what to write."

"Shuo. You no sabi write? You no dey go school? Even me wey no go school sabi write common statement. If you no know wetin you go write oya draw your children dem head for there." His gestures as he spoke were exaggerated and he followed it with a loud hiss. He shifted his gaze to join his colleagues in viewing the football match showing on the screen.

Mother came close and as she spoke I wrote. The potbellied officer looked through the statement when I was done and dismissed us. None of us moved to leave.

"Is that all?" Father asked.

"Wetin again? Except you wan give me money say make I buy malt for all the stress una don give me."

"What are you doing to find the children?" My father pressed on.

"Leave that one for us, na our work. But if you bring money say make we use fuel car e go make work go fast fast."

I looked between all three officers who appeared unperturbed and I felt hopeless. They obviously did not have a plan to catch the kidnapper and didn't even look eager to try.

"So if I give you money now, what will you do to find them?" Father's calm voice belied his temper.

He smiled, his greed blinding him to the disdain oozing out of father's question. "Ahn, that one no be problem. We go go their school early momo tomorrow go put fear for that teacher body till she talk true wetin do your pikin."

"God!" I cried out in horror. Despite not wanting to, I fell into a chair as my head began spinning. The room and everyone in it blurred. "They don't even know what to do. They are as clueless as we are. God, oh, my children. Please find my children."

My cry drew the attention of the male officer who had his eyes on the TV all along, but I paid no heed to his efforts to silence me.

I cried all through the ride home and for most of the night. It was dawn when fatigue took over and I dozed off only to wake and begin crying again at the thought of where my children were sleeping at the moment and if they had been properly fed.

When I went with Obinna to Greenhill School the following day to ask some questions, I noticed parents giving their children's class teachers pictures and names of those permitted to take their children after school. My children and I had become a lesson for others.

With effort, I pushed back the tears and went on with the business of the day. Aunty Shade sat behind her desk, looking refreshed, the way people do early in the morning before the stress of the day takes its toll. None of the distress displayed the day before remained. It infuriated me and I charged at her, asking questions and demanding to know why she left my children to strangers. Obinna failed in his efforts to calm me and it took two security men to get me out of the class.

When Obinna came out to join me, he told me he had gathered from Shade that the man who took our kids is light skinned with dark patches across his skin. He wore a stud earring in one ear, had his hair in short locks and had a full beard. She said the children had not acted like they were afraid or did not know the man. She also claimed that the man had a written note with my signature on it. That last bit of information shocked me.

We took a detour to the police station to give them what information we gathered from the teacher. In spite of the money my father handed them the night before, the pace at the station was slow. There was no flurry of activities to show that they were working.

It dawned on me that the search was up to us and Obinna said as much. Not wanting to go home to face my entire family, who had all stayed home, we returned to Obinna's parents' home and waited. Aunty Oyedinma and Uncle Silas had cut their stay in Greece short and were on their way back to Nigeria after they were informed of the twins' disappearance.

"Do you suspect anyone?" Obinna sat on the tiled floor, one knee raised to support his elbow and his head resting in his hand.

"I have been thinking but I can't come up with anyone," I answered. "You?" He shook his head and stared down at the floor. There was no time to feel sorry for him, though he looked like he needed it, the children deserved it more. I felt impotent. Where to start from, what lead to pursue, eluded me the more I thought.

"Could it be Kingsley? I know he's around."Obinna asked all of a sudden.

Shock that he would consider that had me running to Kingsley's defence. "I know you don't like him, but he will never do that. Besides, he doesn't fit the description," I refuted vehemently, but as soon as that seed was planted, it took root, germinating into sprigs of doubt. He had mentioned something about the children being a barrier after all and, for hours, I mulled over the possibility of him being responsible for my woes.

Obinna's parents returned home in the afternoon and when evening came, we all gathered at my home. Kingsley had become the foremost suspect in my mind and I mentioned this to Aunty Oyedinma when she asked. She wasted no time in putting a call through to the police.

Aunty Oyedinma's quiet authority fired up the police officers so that two hours later, when we returned to the police station, a battered, half-dressed man was dragged out of a cell to the counter. It took me a while to recognize the man in front of me as Kingsley. He sought me in the midst of my family and his eyes bored into mine.

"Why did you treat him like this?" Obinna's mother, unused to physical violence, no doubt preferring her non-physical punitive methods, balked at Kingsley's pitiful appearance. "Do you realize that is someone's child? Please give him back his clothes now," she ordered in a calm but authoritative voice that had the police officers hurrying to do her bidding.

Taking Kingsley aside, she questioned him alone for a while, then returned to inform the officers in a manner that brooked no argument that she was convinced Kingsley was innocent. She added that she would be taking him home herself so that she could apologize to his parents for the actions of the overzealous officers.

Gathered back at her home at the end of the day, Aunty Oyedinma informed us all that it would not serve us to disrupt our schedules and advised that we continue as normal the next day. Though opposed to her suggestion, I did not speak up because, truly, staying home that day had yielded nothing. Also, her argument that during the course of our regular schedules we might get a clue that could lead to the children's whereabouts made sense. What troubled me was her unfazed demeanour. For a moment, I suspected she was glad the twins were gone so that her son could be free. However, when leaving the house, I turned back to look in through the window and saw her daintily flip a tear off her cheek when she thought she was alone in her parlour. She was troubled too, but even in the midst of the storm she remained resolute. As I've done many times in the past, I resolved to be just like her when I'm older.

Once at school the next day, I no longer thought Aunty Oyedinma's decision was sensible. Obinna had stopped by the house that morning with a taxi so we could go to school together. He held me up as I walked from the house to the taxi because it was almost impossible to walk on my own. The effort it took not to envision my children dead was exhausting and with the dawn of a new day came a decline in the intensity of my hope that they would be found alive and untouched.

Every horror story I ever heard or read assumed reality in my mind, playing out with the face of my children. I imagined them being pounded in a mortar. The thought of them being used for child pornography made me gnash my teeth and curl up. I envisaged their body parts being cut out and I almost lost my mind to anguish. What little positivity I had built, waned. At my most hopeless moment I prayed that, at the very least, their kidnappers would be merciful and make it fast and easy for them. At other times, I refused to think of death and endured the migraine that came as I adamantly pushed the ghoulish thoughts away.

In the car, Obinna produced a stack of printed papers his mother gave him. It was a missing person poster with a picture of the twins and a one-million-naira bounty on each child found. As we drove down Brown Road, the taxi driver grumbled at how many times we asked him to stop so we could paste the posters, but quit complaining when Obinna promised to pay for his time. The information was on radio and television too, according to Obinna. I could not abide any form of entertainment and had not been close to a television or a radio to listen. The drive to UNILAG, which should have taken less than an hour, took almost two hours because we kept pasting the notice even as far as Tejuosho and Yaba, though these places were far from the scene of the crime.

However, all I had to do was step into my class to finally decide that sticking to our schedules was not the best idea. Despite trying my best to imitate Obinna's mother, I could not comport myself with dignity. A number of course mates noticed my countenance and came to ask what was wrong with me, but I only confided in Kosi. When it became impossible to sit still and tears threatened, I left my class to paste some of the posters within the school premises. I assumed it was a waste of efforts yet I continued because it made me feel useful.

I had just re-entered the class when a junior colleague came to inform me that Professor Okoro wanted me in his office immediately.

Barely had I closed the door to Abike's office when Professor Okoro began speaking to me. Abike was not in sight and Okoro was sitting on her seat. His measured tone flashed a warning signal that there was a problem.

"I noticed you're unusually close to Abike," he said.

It was more a question than a statement of fact and I had no idea how to answer so I didn't say anything.

"I know your coursemates avoid her, so how come you two get along well?" he asked.

I shrugged. "I'm not sure how that happened sir."

"I'm asking because I'm trying to get to the root of this," he said, lifting sheets of papers that I recognized as the answer sheets used for exams.

I reached for the papers but he held them away from me.

"Can you explain to me what your exam sheet is doing in my secretary's drawer," he said.

"Oh my God!" was all I could say as it dawned on me that my missing script had been in Abike's drawer all this time and she had me running around, looking for it.

"There's only one way I can explain this," Professor Okoro said. "You were not sure of your answers so, you left the hall with extra exam sheets, completed it in your free time and gave Abike to help you switch it with the exam sheet you submitted. Am I right?"

"What? No sir," I began, trying to explain myself but he interrupted me.

"That seems like the only plausible explanation, though I can't imagine Abike agreeing to something like that." He frowned and considered. "How much did you pay for her to agree to something like this?"

My heart did a slight jiggle as I realized how quickly this could turn against me. All Abike has to do is to agree that Professor Okoro's theory is right and he would believe her. She was in trouble already, the exam sheet was found in her drawer, and I knew she wouldn't hesitate to drag me down with her.

"Sir, you've got it all wrong. That's my exam script I've been looking for. I had a missing script in the course."

"If you were not involved in any shady business, why didn't you apply to have your missing script addressed?"

"Sir, I applied this Monday, the first day school resumed."

"Do I look like a fool to you?" Spittle flew out with the words, his eyes a blazing fury. "Every letter that gets to Abike's desk gets to me before the end of the day. How can you make such false claims?" He pointed an angry finger at me. "Do you realize you are implicating a woman who has worked for me for almost five years without so much as a dent to her work ethics?"

Immediately, I broke down in tears, yowling like a baby without shame. This outburst elicited a look of disdain from him.

"And to think I went out of my way to offer you this admission. Is this how you've been excelling in all your other courses? Tears will not help you now. This is a crime that will cost you your admission."

"I didn't do anything wrong." My raised voice carried none of the respect everyone usually accorded him. I realized I needed to behave before I went too far, but the rage of the past few days tumbled out with my protest.

"Abike told me she has given you my application letter. I even have an extra copy of it. I didn't cheat. My children have been missing since Tuesday and the last thing I want is more trouble. I'm tired. I'm just tired." There was no strength left when I was done. I felt drained and hung my head, too numb to feel even fear. Then as the silence stretched, there was enough time to calm down and the fear returned with such vengeance that I almost wet myself.

The paper stuck to his elbow as he lifted his arm from the desk and made a sweeping motion for me to continue. "I'm listening."

I explained everything, from how I realized my result was missing on Monday, to how I was unable to follow up the case of the missing result because my children were kidnapped from their school.

"Unfortunately, Abike isn't here to speak for herself. She's been away from her desk for too long now. Where is that girl anyway?" He turned toward the door angrily as if doing that will make his secretary appear.

He lifted the offending paper. "I came to search her drawer for a file I needed from her and found this. I can't make any conclusions until you bring me your own copy of the application letter with her signature to show that she received a copy from you. I will sort this out with her when she returns. You can go now."

He lifted his brow when I made no move to leave. I ignored the phone vibrating in my bag.

"Sir, she didn't sign my copy."

"So how are you going to prove that she collected the original? You could leave here and go print a copy now to present to me."

"No need sir. I have the copy here." The phone beeped again as I opened my purse to bring out the folded letter. He frowned and shook his head when he went through the letter.

"Something is definitely not right," he said.

Chapter Eighteen

Something is not right here. Where are you?

Outside, I tried to call Obinna to understand the meaning of the text message he sent to me then I realized I did not have airtime. The corridor outside of Professor Okoro's office branched out to three other passages and I took the right one as I headed for Obinna's class. I stopped within sight of his faculty block and stared. A rowdy crowd was gathered in front of the building. Heads poked out of windows, both upstairs and downstairs, gawking at the commotion. Most of those outside shoved through the sea of bodies, trying to get to the centre to ascertain the cause.

Reluctant to get involved, I rounded the block then took the back stairs. Suddenly realizing his message could mean that he was involved in the chaos outside, my pace quickened and I was soon running. Heads jerked up when I flew into his class.

"Where's Obinna?" I asked the nearest person. She spread her hands and shook her head.

I joined those at the window, searching the heads below for Obinna. My sight settled on two uniformed men struggling to hold on to a tough looking guy who was bent on making it impossible for them. He shook himself free at some point and would have escaped, but for the bodies blocking his path. When they finally held him down he managed to turn his head backward to pin someone behind him with eyes that looked like fiery orbs. I followed the path of those eyes and they landed on a female. Abike. I gasped, then noticed her hands were behind her back too, held there by a woman in mufti.

Professor Okoro was certainly fast, I thought. Fresh fury rose from my stomach into my mouth so that I almost screamed insults down on her, but my gaze shifted and met Obinna's in the crowd. Looking at him, I knew the commotion had nothing to do with Professor Okoro or my result.

For the second time that day, Obinna and I were together in a taxi plying the road we took earlier, in reverse. Our joined hands rested between us as he spoke about the drama that took place in front of his faculty building.

He had been upstairs, unable to concentrate too, then he looked out of the window at the poster he put on a pole that morning. Two people stood in front of it. He paid little attention to them until one hand shot out and stabbed repeatedly at the line on which was written the reward for whoever found the children. From their body language, they were arguing and it was heated. He almost turned away, but something on the boy's ear glinted in the bright midday sun, causing him to give the scene more attention. That was when he noticed the earring, locked hair and full beard. He also noticed who the female with him was and his suspicion peaked.

"Reason told me it was farfetched, but instinct said otherwise, especially after I remembered something Abike had said; that Chika and Chuka were standing between us."

"What? Wait. Back up. She said what? When?"

He lifted his hand to snap his fingers repeatedly, a gesture that said it was a long time ago.

"She somehow got the idea that I was into her and mentioned that she was available. When I told her I didn't see her in that way and felt nothing for her, she refused to accept it and said I was refusing her only because of the children and you."

"How come you never mentioned this?"

"I thought about it, believe me, but then I figured she didn't know their school so it couldn't possibly be her."

Realization dawned then. "God! I destroyed my life by myself. I told her the name of their school just recently. I even told her their class."

"Don't blame yourself. We can't be sure yet that they have anything to do with it, though the guy fits the description Aunty Shade gave. And the way they acted in front of my block says a lot."

"I hope they are the ones so our search will be over once and for all," I said.

"Ah wait now, I haven't even finished giving you the gist." He slanted his body to face me. "As I was still deciding what to think after I saw them arguing, I called Abike's name and the force with which she jumped showed she had something to hide. Next thing I knew she was dragging the guy, but he refused to go with her. He pulled back his hand and the impact threw her to the ground. When she stood she just went crazy, snatched the paper off the pole and, after tearing it into pieces, threw it at him. That was when I knew this was not ordinary again, so I called school security and mum."

With a new and promising lead to pursue, anticipation replaced the sorrow that had lodged in my heart for days. More drama unfolded from questioning Abike and her male accomplice. Before nightfall, they had given enough information to satisfy the most insatiable of the journalists who gathered in front of Soloki Police Station like hungry wolves.

Three more people were brought into custody in relation to the kidnap: the grandmother of Abike's male accomplice, a middle-aged woman running an unregistered orphanage, and her husband.

That same day, as the hands of the clock neared midnight, my impatience grew as I waited with Obinna and our parents in Uncle Silas' car. My arms hungered to hold my children, but each lead led to another and I hoped this lead would be the final one. At about quarter past twelve that night, I heard the siren of a police car and looked out of the car to see a police van swerve into the front of the station and park. Out of the open back of the van came a woman, crying and adjusting her wrapper over her nightgown.

She kept repeating, "I didn't steal them o. I adopted them."

A brooding man was pushed from behind by a policeman so he stumbled as he jumped down from the van, but caught himself before he hit the ground. They were led into the station.

My family was out of the car as soon as the door to the passenger's side of the police van opened and Officer Ngozi came out, her arms curved around two toddlers. The time it took me to run across the road and reach her could not have been more than ten seconds but it felt like more. Hope and fear pumped my heart, propelling me forward. I felt as if they could vanish forever if I got there a second later.

The moment I reached Officer Ngozi, I snatched the twins from her arms. Then I was hugging them and greedily sniffing their baby scent which I had missed so much. I felt the arms of Obinna and our families surround us and my world was complete.

Chapter Nineteen

With my children back home, no member of our families – mine and Obinna's – wanted to be away from them for long.

The kids were withdrawn from Greenhill Nursery and Primary school and Aunty Oyedinma employed a nanny to watch them at her home during the day while we all went about our daily activities. As soon as my lectures for the day were over, I hurried to Obinna's parent's home to relieve the nanny and return home with my children.

Obinna and his parents spent almost every evening at my home, fussing over the twins. None of us attended the court proceedings involving the kidnappers of my children but we read about it in the newspapers Uncle Silas brought home from work. The case had garnered national attention and every newspaper in Lagos had a journalist following up on the court hearing.

The day a verdict was reached, one of the major papers had on the front page a picture of Abike, cuffed and wailing as she was led out of the courtroom, her male accomplice who abducted the kids from their school in tow. It was also from the papers that we learnt that the young man in question is called Ademola, a man who assisted his grandmother in the shop where she sold snacks and drinks on the grounds of Unilag. He had tried unsuccessfully for years to win Abike's affection. When she went to him with the plan to kidnap the twins, she promised to accept his plea to start an amorous relationship if he executed the plan properly.

To make the plan work and have Abike for himself, Ademola had involved his grandmother, who, in turn, got her friend, the woman running the illegal orphanage, involved. It was discovered that the couple who adopted my children were totally oblivious to the crime committed. They were simply a naïve, desperate couple who were conned by the orphanage and as such, they were acquitted.

Abike and Ademola both got ten years in prison each. The couple in charge of the illegal orphanage got sentenced to a total of twenty six years in jail. Ademola's grandmother, who got her cut from the sale of the children, slumped and died before a verdict was reached, hence 'escaping justice' as the newspapers termed it. I did not see her death as an escape of justice. If anything, I knew she would not last more than a month in jail had she lived long enough to be sent there.

It was also revealed during the trial that it was the letter Abike had encouraged me to write to the Exams and Records department, to allow someone search for my missing result, that Ademola had presented to Aunty Shade. The letter had my signature so Greenhill School said there was no reason to punish Shade for letting a stranger take Chika and Chuka from school.

Their evil scheme might have gone as planned and my children would have become the children of the couple who adopted them, while I'd spend the rest of my life grieving, had Ademola not gotten greedy when he saw the generous reward for each child found. He tried to get Abike to abandon her need for vengeance and permit him to tip off the police to the children's whereabouts so they could claim the money. He had a plan that would keep them from being seen as suspects in the kidnap. However, Abike was not doing it for the money hence she remained adamant. The argument that ensued thereof was what led to their exposure.

When normalcy returned to my life, I went to Kingsley's house to apologise for naming him as a suspect and for the ill-treatment he endured from the police officers, but was told he had returned to school. When he came home for the holidays he gave me a wide berth and we have since become strangers.

On the other hand, united in sorrow and in triumph, Obinna and I became closer, almost inseparable. What Abike had hoped would tear us apart had brought us even closer and increased our love and respect for each other. I had no more fears for my future - whether alone or with Obinna in it - the worst had happened and I triumphed and came out of it whole. I knew I would be alright.

Epilogue

Life can be planned but there is no guarantee that it will go exactly as outlined. More often than not, events unfold that we do not expect, leading us in a different direction from where we set out to be.

My life had taken a detour, through several downturns, but it brought me to the exact place where I always wanted to be.

I had made so many wrong choices, choices against which I will advise my children in the future. I had broken all the rules; had children before marriage, children fathered by onye mba. I wonder if I will choose to change anything if I have to do it over again.

As though he can read my thoughts, Obinna asks from his position behind me, "Given another chance, will you do things differently?"

I consider his question for a long time before I answer. "Maybe if I had to do it again I might wait till the time is right to have a baby, but of what use is regret? Right now I want my life no other way." As I utter the words, I realize I truly mean them.

I do not want second chances or a better life. Regret is a waste of efforts. I am in love with a man who loves me, I have children who bring new joy to life with every new day and I have a great job waiting for me as soon as I'm done with the compulsory National Youth Service Corps.

The job had been Professor Okoro's doing. I surprised not just myself and my family, but him as well when I graduated with a first class degree. I got an offer from my alma mater to resume as a junior lecturer immediately after completion of NYSC. I am perfectly content, for myself and also for my siblings who are all doing well.

Ama is getting ready to leave the country immediately after NYSC for her Masters degree program in the University of Reading; the same university where Nnenna is studying as an undergraduate. Ujunwa, Olanma, Ifeyichi and Chukwuemeka are progressing also. I am thankful that the example I set did not influence them negatively.

"What about you?" I search Obinna's face for signs of regret.

He shakes his head. "We've had the worst time of it in the past, but I'm happy with where we are now. We've paid the price and I have no complaints about reaping the benefits." His hand caresses the slight swell of my stomach as I sit on our bed nestled between his thighs.

It is the fourth month of our marriage and the second year anniversary of the day our children were rescued. Our trials brought us together and increased our appreciation of each other, so that as soon as I graduated, we did not need the approval of society to decide we wanted to get married. Admitted, we are young, but we have been through enough together and if those had not torn us apart, nothing else could.

Our experience had toughened us beyond our years and prepared us for marriage and the future. Obinna, who has been working since his second year in university, secured a job with the same company immediately after his NYSC year. Though most people believe that we are able to live on our own because of Obinna's parents' generosity, the truth is that he had been no ordinary student. He started quite early, studying, working, saving and is now able to support our young family alone, obstinately refusing the offer of help from his family.

Mr and Mrs Onwuka, having observed how well their son is doing on his own, finally stopped pushing and are simply content with looking for every opportunity to visit or to have Chika and Chuka over at theirs.

The twins are over at their grandparents' at the moment, to my relief. I never knew a time would come when I'd be glad to have them gone for a short while, to have a moment of respite, but at almost five years old, they are excessively hyperactive and, though a pleasure to watch, they tire me out sometimes, especially with another baby coming.

With pleasure, I think about how different this pregnancy is from the last. I am carrying this one with pride and none of the fear that had been present the last time. Most importantly, I have the man I love with me to share every moment of it. I am eagerly looking forward to the birth and so is he.

"What if it turns out to be twins again?" His thumb smoothes the thinking lines etched between my brows.

"We'll have to wait till tomorrow to find out."

"Let's bet on the outcome. Whoever wins - "

"Whoever loses will do the cooking every day for two months," I interject.

"No way! That's not even a deal because you know that I won't be able to let you do all the cooking while you are pregnant, even if you lose."

"That's a good deal in my opinion." My smile comes easily, knowing it is a win-win situation for me.

"I bet on twins again," he says.

"It will be a single pregnancy," I predict, but it doesn't matter. Single or multiple, I am a very happy woman. I have proven that one misstep isn't the end of one's life.

"I love you so much it's hard to ever imagine feeling otherwise." Obinna declares suddenly, his voice hoarse with emotion that is infectious.

"Feel otherwise and have Nnenna skin you alive," I warn and he shivers in mock terror. This makes us laugh uncontrollably.

"I love you too."

I link my hands with his where they rest on my belly rubbing the bump that will soon be a living child and a part of our story. A story that started one rainy day...

THE END